Casualty Of War

Pamela Turton

Pamela Turton has asserted her right under the Copyright, Designs and Patents Act 1988 to be identified as the author of this work.

This novel is a work of fiction. All characters in this publication are fictitious, and any resemblance to real persons, living or dead, is purely coincidental.

Other Works by Pamela Turton

Novels:

Stalkbook

Blue is the Object

The Life Coach Less Travelled

Selling Short

So Sister

Poetry:

Spanish Steps, Sources and Seasons

Christ's Passion in Poetry and Perspective

Non-Fiction:

A Handbook of Happy Habits

Find out more : <u>pamelaturton.com</u>

In war, truth is the first casualty.

- Aeschylus, Greek dramatist, 5th Century BCE

Summer 2017

Chapter 1

As she stoops, batting away clouds of dust, her headscarf makes her look more like a Middle Eastern village housewife than a glamorous Foreign Correspondent for H. I. 4 News, although when she looks up into the camera I see she is wearing a helmet. The unnecessary subtitle reads "loud blast", and between the bangs we hear urgent, panicked footsteps crunching on rock and dirt. "F*****g hell" the censored text reads beneath the blurred frames of the skewed camera. Thea Bridger, the intrepid journalist, swears again; breathless and confused. There are glimpses of the backs and shoulders of unidentified figures running amidst the scrubland. Thea yells to a man off-screen, pleading to him to stay with her. The team regroups, huddling by the frame of a roofless structure.

Although we can hear her words, the caption confirms them: "He's been hit. F*****g hell." I fill in the blanks for her, three times, because now the subtitle is informing us that "a civilian activist who has joined us has been hit by shrapnel." I recognise his name from their dialogue then his features as Thea and her companion attend to his wound. I know his face because the so-called civilian activist who prefers to call himself an on-the-ground journalist has filmed many interviews with fighters he calls rebels. One of his interviewees was strapped up with a suicide belt, another was a vocal, emotional Saudi cleric; a fanatical advocate of the mujahideen in Syria. I also know that Thea's civilian activist is on the US terrorist target list, because I like to check this stuff out and, hell, the guy has complained himself about being targeted on Twitter. Hell all right.

Thea Bridger takes up the commentary, explaining that her press team which she says was clearly marked, was "deliberately targeted by a Syrian regime drone." I wonder how it picked out markings that I could not and how her team got there in the first place. A long-bearded man in black zooms into view, flinging out clouds of smoke and powdered stone on his motorbike as the reporter speaks of innocent civilians being targeted. There is little sign of life in the rubbled, scrubby semi-rural landscape she is navigating, few of the rebels she refers to, or the jihadist hordes other reporters warn are in control of that area. There is another explosion. This time the cameraman captures Thea fleeing, gripping her microphone like a baton, conveying the sounds of her intense distress and physical exertion. I am struck by her bravery, and also in her abaya her resemblance to a game but unfit middle-aged teacher taking part in the sack race at my primary school. Not used to it. It takes skill.

The context of the news report and the scenario took me back to a previous report by an American mainstream news channel, in another north-east Syrian town not far from the one where Thea Bridger was placed. The narrative was similar, as was the female reporter's dress and untypical lack of make-up, but she was thinner, younger and more agile in her floor-length gown. Back in the flashy, glassy newsroom she fleshed out her scoop sporting a tight-fitting dress, professionally applied make-up and fluffy blonde hair. In a plaintive, nasal whine she asserted the atrocities of the Syrian regime. Stone-throwing.

The stark contrast of the reporting of a young, independent Canadian journalist came to mind. She records different stories from the voices of Syrian civilians she encounters, as she wanders around the streets of Government-held areas. Some are still in the state of sad, shattered ruin, others in the hopeful stages of rebuilding. Family homes pocked and punctured by mortars, their hearts blown out by human loss, and ancient souks decapitated by modern weapons. A formidable Citadel carries its tale of centuries of defiance and fortitude into the twenty-first century. In her vest top and jeans, her ponytail swinging, she and the young people she talks to remind me of our own friends. She speaks quite a bit of Arabic and smiles a lot. I admire her courage but mostly she impresses me because, although she lacks the status and security of a regular paycheck from media magnates, she is free and I sense her honesty. I relate to her quest for the truth.

Truth is beauty, beauty truth. Sometimes, not often, I have had a feeling for what Keats was getting at, but right then I could only think of the kind of truth I seemed to be being presented with; ugly, inconvenient, convenient and conflicting. How could we ever get to the bottom of it when the bottom line is the pointless suffering of so many people? On my phone I opened the Twitter feed of Thea Bridger's civilian activist to see what he had to say for himself. He, unlike H.I.4 News, was keen to Tweet about his involvement in their news report. With candid bravado he played down his injury from the shelling. He described the incident as an interruption to their on-the-ground reporting by an army tank; whose he does not say.

Grappling with the discrepancies in these apparent truths about war was giving me a headache and I needed a distraction. There was plenty to choose from right there in my comparatively peaceful part of the world. For a start my own flat looked like a war zone, which I needed to do something about before Freya arrived. Hunger was a diversion; my need to eat was compelling but my fridge and food cupboards were empty. I had no drastic excuse such as sanctions; only lack of planning and perhaps a little laziness. I sent a text message to Gilly requesting emergency supplies; the least he could do was pick up some bread and milk on his way after the effort I had put in on his final assignment. Just as I'd started to feel free from the shackles of University he enlisted my help to save him with his. At least I could get something out of it since he changed his course from Advertising to Film Production after first year, which could come in useful for our plans. But I was frustrated because my own work was done and I resented being stuck in this airless flat, with the sun shining in, highlighting the dust.

"God, you're letting things go a bit aren't you mate?"

Gilly pushed an empty fruit juice carton and some dirty dishes aside, to make space to plonk down the loaf and milk. He'd brought eggs as well so for the time being he was forgiven.

"Maybe if I wasn't stuck in here, tied up doing work for you, I might be able to get on top of things. Besides, if Em wasn't constantly tidying up your place and your Mum wasn't willing to shell out for a cleaner to muck it out on a regular basis, you wouldn't be living in such a palace anyway."

"Fair point, mate. Fair point."

Gilly was conciliatory, realising it was best not to push it since I was doing him such a big favour. "Sorry, bud. You know I'm massively grateful to you for helping me out with this. I don't know, I just got stuck with it. It was doing my head in. You're a really good mate as well as being super smart."

He grinned and punched my shoulder.

"Yeah well, flattery is not going to get you everywhere here. Brewing up, cooking up a big fat omelette and some toast will, while I finish this paragraph. Then maybe I can tidy things up a bit."

"On it," he said, tugging out the frying pan from a shelf after banging a few cupboard doors, and holding it up to his face for inspection. "I'd better just give this a swill. By the way, how's it going?"

"How is what going?" I smiled to soften my churlish response.

"The assignment."

"Your assignment should be finished soon, mate. And it might have been done earlier if I hadn't had to correct so many typos, and end up rewriting sodding half of it."

Gilly shook his head and laughed, patting me on the shoulder he did not punch.

"I owe you one," he said and blew on the feathers hanging by the frame of the kitchen window. "What's this?"

"It's a dream catcher. Freya made it for me."

"What's that about then?"

"It's a Native American Indian thing. The web bit is supposed to trap your bad dreams. I think the feathers let your good dreams through, but I can't remember exactly. Freya will tell you."

"Freya, yeah." Gilly laughed. "Nice. But what's it doing in the kitchen?"

"Don't ask me, she just likes making them. And I've had to put it up there because Grizzle likes attacking it. I have got a bigger one in the bedroom over my bed. I'm sure she'd love to make you one if you asked her nicely."

"Ha ha. Okay. First you need to tell me if your dreams have got better."

I tilted my hand left to right. "So so."

"Maybe they'll improve after you've filled your boots with my more than decent omelette. Come and trough, then I'll do the dishes for you."

"Wow, we are in a generous mood today."

My own mood was brighter after the food, especially since Gilly actually cooked for me and kept his promise to do the washing up, albeit with a lot of clinking, clanking and a bit of swearing. When he had finished, I had tidied up all his paperwork, vacuumed and had started some slapdash dusting.

"Do you want a hand?" He picked up the little tray of

crystals Freya had arranged for me on the coffee table, and began puffing out the tiny debris between the stones. "What time did you say you'd get to the church?"

"Well I said by three so I've still got an hour. I said I'd give them a hand for a couple of hours. Freya has been there since around nine this morning. At least she and some of the others can eat, although I know she doesn't like to do it in front of them."

"I don't know what you're talking about mate. Who can't eat and why can't Freya eat in front of them?"

"Ramadan. More than half the volunteers are fasting now. I don't know how they do it on long, warm days like this. I've got a lot of respect for them."

Gilly shook his head, breathing out an almost–whistle.

"That takes some doing man. Anyway, if you want I'll take you and help out until you're done. I haven't got any plans for the rest of the day and it will be good to see how it's all going."

"Hey, you haven't been taking happy pills this morning have you?"

"Nope, just being my usual magnanimous self. That's the right word isn't it? Like I said, I owe you and I'm pretty excited about this project."

From under the pile of papers I had just tidied away I pulled out a local newspaper.

"Did you see the article about us in here?"

I opened it up and pointed to the image dominating the page over the headline: 'Student Charity Cycle Race April 2017 Raises Record Cash For War-Torn Country.'

"Let's have a look. My Mum took my copy, though I think Em's got one somewhere. Amazing to think that was less than two months ago, and everything that's been achieved since then. Can't wait to see the wheels."

"Me too. Atif texted me last night to say the ambulances were almost ready and he was hoping they'd arrive this morning."

"Fantastic. Let's go."

I was happy to take up Gilly's offer of a lift, not just because the Merc is way more comfortable than my Kia; there was bound to be much more in the fuel tank.

"I don't know if I told you that I had a chat with that guy from the Chronicle who did the article on us about the Charity Cycle Race. Can you actually believe that he's been doing that job for twenty years?" I said, as Gilly turned the air conditioning on and I leaned back for the ride.

"Maybe it suits him to keep things cosy and local. Pootling about in other people's lives without the drama. Time to pick the kids up from school and mow the lawn all that kind of stuff."

"Yeah. Maybe I can't relate to that lack of ambition from where I am now, you know? It almost makes me shudder to think I could get stuck in that kind of set-up. I've been giving it a lot of thought. I mean, if our plans take off and we can do the kind of work we want to do, that would be fantastic."

"Absolutely. Edgy investigative journalism. What I really fancy is getting to travel about and film in really neat locations, hooking up with some really top, cool, crazy people."

"First we need the funding and the opportunities. Where to start?"

"Dad's been really good about supplying the equipment and all that, but I doubt he's willing to invest more at this point. Maybe if he sees us making a go of it later."

"I'm really grateful to him for giving us a start in the first place, for sure. Next week I'm going to make it a priority to start researching funding, grants and all that. We still need a hook to get going."

"Have you thought about alternatives if it takes a while for us to build it up? We've got to get income, put food on the table and all that. At least I don't have to pay for the rent but still. I don't fancy tightening my belt because I'm skint."

"Well, apart from taking pictures of schoolkids with certificates, prize courgettes at the local allotment and interviewing old age pensioners and whoever about the effects of Austerity, possibly my worst fear is pushing paper, fetching coffee and writing pointless, half-read pieces that haven't been spiked by some newspaper-owning plutocrat."

Gilly laughed, taking one hand off the wheel to slap my thigh. "Could be worse things, man. You've got to have faith."

Chapter 2

The volunteers at the InterFaith project for Syria at Carmel Church were in full flow when we arrived. The chairs that seat the diminishing but faithful congregation for services, and the usual religious celebrations, were stacked beside the walls to make room for the heap of bundles, boxes and bags of food, toiletries and other necessities. At first it was hard to pick out Freya and our friends amongst the moving waves of people holding out their arms to give or receive, passing on the gifts one to another in organised lines of industry. Men and women, varying in age, race and dress, worked together in harmony. Chatting and laughing, they created order from the chaos of contributions, occasionally stopping to wipe the sweat from their eyes. Some were in T-shirts and shorts; the Muslims wore mainly black, the women in hijab and long gowns in respect of the holy month. Dressed in the same style but in her signature colour of pale blue, a statue of Mary holding her Babe-in-arms smiled over Freya and Saffi, who were stacking packs of disposable nappies in a corner of the room.

We were about to make our way over to them when a sparse-haired, tall, gangly man with spectacles and a 'no holds barred' grin blocked our path with an open-armed gesture of welcome. At the neck of his pink polo shirt he wore a white clerical collar. He introduced himself as the Minister of Carmel Church. "Have you come to volunteer?"

We said we had, and he explained what each of the different groups was doing around the room. Joining his palms and releasing them, he spoke with evident, breathless satisfaction. His tight, spitting consonants suggested South Africa. He was interrupted by a mug of tea being slotted into his open hands by a shiny-faced, plump lady in a colourful turban and a wide, orange silk kaftan with an indigo tribal pattern at the chest and sleeves, which rippled in harmony with her movements.

"Ah, here's my wife looking after me as usual. Four more willing hands my dear."

Before any of us could say anything I felt a slap on my back. It was Atif.

"Hey, good to see you guys."

As we turned he grabbed both of our hands with warmth in his lively, black-liquid eyes. More often than not they sparkled with a playfulness that was reflected in his grin; a contrast to his deep, resonant manner of speaking.

"Well pleased you guys could make it today."

"Me too. Did Gilly tell you we've got some free time so we can help out today?"

"No, that's great. How long have you got?"

"Well, what time you thinking of packing it in?"

"Not later than seven. That will give us time to get home and cleaned up, and have a bit of a rest before Iftar."

"We'll stay 'til at least six, and Gilly is giving me and Freya a lift home."

"Okay, that's good. If you look around, Freya and Saffi and some of the other women are sorting out baby stuff, toiletries and the lighter stuff. The guys are mainly shifting the heavier loads; rice, chickpeas, dried beans, flour and all that kind of thing."

"There's so much of it, and it keeps coming," I said, pointing to the big arched doorway where two Asian men were shuffling in, carrying a large plastic sack between them, alongside a woman holding two large supermarket bags. "Who's given all this stuff?"

"Mainly local business people, not just people from the Christian and Muslim communities." Atif placed his palm over his heart and patted it. "To be honest, we've been overwhelmed by how kind people are. A lot of individuals and small charitable groups in the area have got involved as well."

Gilly tapped Atif's shoulder. "Bro, before we get going,

14

any chance we can see the ambulances?"

Atif tapped his forehead with the heel of his hand.

"Man, I swear my mind gets fuzzy by this time of the day. They arrived this morning, all ten of them. Pretty exciting, eh? I don't know how they could have slipped my mind. You must be dying to check them out? Follow me."

"Where are you keeping them?" Gilly said.

"We've struck lucky there. The Police Training Centre which is practically next door has a big car park that is only ever half full, so we've got permission to keep them there which is perfect because it's so secure too."

He turned to the Minister. "Tim," he said, "Gilly and Dylan here were part of the Student Charity Cycle Race and had a lot to do with getting us the ambulances."

"Magnificent work." Minister Tim put his arm round Atif's shoulder. "Yes, the world needs more young men and women of your calibre."

"Our pleasure sir," Gilly said in the humble tone that annoys me although I know he means well, and he has a compulsive need to exercise his charm. "It seems a small contribution compared to the team who are actually going to take part in the convoy."

"Without the ambulances there would be no convoy." The kind face which owned the authoritative voice came into view.

Tim clapped his hands. "Good timing, Javid, my man. This is my other half so to speak." He chuckled at his little joke. "That is to say, this is the Imam from our local mosque whom, delightfully I must say, has been our main partner in this project."

"Can I get your cup of tea or anything, Javid?" The minister's wife clasped her hands to her mouth as soon as the words came out.

The Imam waved her apology and her offer away with a gentle raise of his palm.

"Not today thank you, Janet."

Minister Tim placed his own mug of tea between her

open hands and closed her fingers around it with his own, whispering "Maybe later, my dear."

The two men of the cloth walked away together, one dark, small and stout, the other pallid, tall and lean, engaged in amicable chatter. Janet scurried away with the mug.

Atif steered us through the heaps of donations and sweating volunteers out into the street, where the air was almost as close as the atmosphere inside the hall, with a lethargic breeze to ease it.

"Hang on, I'll just grab some keys so you can have a look inside."

He ran back into the church, returning a minute later jangling the keys. He led us past some high metal railings through an open gate, at the side of which a man sitting inside a booth, wearing just a yellow vest marked SECURITY over his tattooed torso, waved us through with a nod and a thumbs up sign. Atif returned the friendly gesture.

"Cheers pal." To us he said, "They're at the back of the building."

We passed several police cars, some unmarked, and a few vans with various designations and turned left to see a whole row of ten parking bays. Each was occupied by a gleaming white, chequered and chevroned, reconditioned ambulance.

"There you go," said Atif, pausing with his hands on his hips in a state of obvious satisfaction. "What do you think guys? You must be really proud of yourselves."

"Oh man, that's really something," I said, performing a happy two-step on the tarmac. "I mean, we were totally made up to achieve our target of five of them, but it's really something else to see them for ourselves."

Gilly held his palms up like a sun god for both of us to slap them in triumph.

"Sweet."

We ran our hands over the body of the first ambulance

in the row as if it was an exotic creature we were privileged to pet. Atif pointed out where the NHS lettering had been removed, now covered over with the logo of the InterFaith project. He unlocked the doors and slid back the one at the side. Inside, the vehicle had been gutted; all the medical equipment had been removed apart from a small, wall mounted first-aid kit, a fire extinguisher, two folding seats at the back and a narrow platform bench. Atif told us how most of the space would be filled with supplies, leaving a small area for sleeping on the floor which he demonstrated by lying down.

"So the drivers will take turns to drive and rest. We'll have a thin foam mattress here, sleeping bags and pillows. We'll stop at motorway services sometimes and catch some kip there, and we'll sleep on the ferry of course."

Gilly shook his head. "What do you do about food?"

"On the convoy trips I've been on – this will be my fourth – we've had basic camping equipment to boil water, fry eggs, cook rice and beans, that kind of thing. We take some basics and usually buy fresh bread, cheese, fruit and vegetables wherever and whenever we can."

I clambered into the front, settled myself in the driver's seat and held the wheel.

"I'm feeling really excited about this. I mean, it's not just a really good thing that you guys are doing, and I know it could be dangerous, but it's a fantastic adventure too."

Atif squeezed in next to me followed by Gilly.

"Yeah, all of the drivers have done this before; for about six of them this will be their seventh run. Apart from being uncomfortable at times, the lack of sleep, and sometimes a hassle with paperwork, most of the hiccups have been minor; a decent diet, keeping the petrol tank full enough, flat tyres and that kind of problem. It's really important to have a good network on the ground inside the area we're travelling to."

Atif nodded his head a few times to emphasise his last point, and we copied him to show we understood.

"I'm almost wishing I could go with you," I said, after we had jumped out and Atif was locking the ambulance.

Gilly laughed. "Seriously?"

"Seriously. By the way Atif, do you know which of these were bought from our fundraising?"

"Nah, not sure bro. You'd have to ask my cousin Mo. He was the one who sourced these." He laughed. "He's actually a trainee solicitor from Leicester and a whizz with mechanics, would you believe? Man of many talents is our Mo. When we go back inside I'll introduce you to him."

Back inside the church hall, before we did the rounds with Atif, I crept up behind Freya, placed my hands on her bare upper arms and whispered "Boo" in her left ear. She started, dropping the bulky package of toilet rolls she was holding and almost tripping on the hem of her dress. Despite her uncovered arms, I thought it was like Freya to think about what she would wear to fit in.

"Dylan, you eejit," she shouted in a joyful voice, slapping my wrist. "When did you get here?" "

"Not long ago. Gilly brought me and we've been to look at the ambulances. Fantastic. We're going to help now for a couple of hours."

"Well, get to work man and do us all some good. Hey Saffi, look girl, we've got some reinforcements."

Saffi pushed her bundle into place and came over to say hello. Normally brimming, her energy level was clearly low, and under her eyes on her bright, pretty face were shadows.

Atif called me over to where he was standing with Gilly, and a group of four Asian men who appeared to be of a similar age to us. He introduced us to Mo, another cousin and two close friends of his who would all be driving in the convoy. He then took us over to four other men who were working with a forklift truck. One of the men, with high, lupine cheekbones, a beard that reached his collarbones and dark sunglasses, watched as we approached. As we reached his group he scowled, pulled a mobile phone from the pocket of his loose trousers and hurried away, out of our sight and earshot. Atif raised a hand and opened his mouth as if to call him back, but put his hands into his pockets and shrugged instead.

"That's Saif. We only met him today, although Zaheel knows his cousin. He told him we were short of two drivers still, and the cousin got in touch with Saif, who has been on seven convoys to Syria already and was keen to get involved."

I watched Saif's back as he slipped into the shadows with his phone to his ear.

"We've not really had chance to get to know him yet. He seems a pretty quiet kind of guy," Atif said, turning back to the group.

We became acquainted with the other three, each of them greeting us with a strong handshake, kind words and a pat on the arm for our contribution to the cause. Gilly stayed to work with the forklift team while I went off with Atif and Mo to shift stacks of rice. I got off to a hilarious start by skidding on a dry puddle of spilled grains, which was a bit embarrassing until I noticed how it lifted the mood of the nearby workers. Having a good laugh must have helped to take their minds off the strain of heavy work in that heat, during their fast.

The late afternoon grew cooler, supporting our exertions and helping the time pass more quickly. It felt good to me to be working my muscles for a worthwhile outcome; to be linked in effort and spirit to a team like this. Atif, as usual, was good company but after a few hours he was flagging.

"I think I'm going to have to call it a day bro," he said with a slight bowed head-shake of defeat.

Gilly must have noticed our slowing down, because he glanced at his watch, took off the thick gloves he had been wearing and strolled over.

"It's six-thirty now Dylan. Are you okay to make a move? I'm actually starving mate. I could eat a horse."

Noticing my eyes rolling he looked over at Atif then tapped both cheeks with his fingers. "Sorry. Jesus, sorry. Sorry."

Atif seemed to be entertained, which is more than I could say for myself.

"Don't worry about it bro," he said.

Outside, waiting by the car for Freya, Gilly apologised again. "At least I didn't say I could eat a pig."

"No, there is that, you numpty."

Chapter 3

On the drive back to my place Freya exhausted us even more with her exuberant chatter about the day's work at the church; the comings and goings, all the small and bigger conversations.

"Aren't you tired?" Gilly said as we waited for the traffic lights to turn green. "I'm knackered and I've only done a few hours. How can you be this lively after nine hours solid?"

"Yes how can you?" I gave her arm a playful pinch. Laughing with us she called us "Lightweights." She looked out of the window, watching a greengrocer pause in the packing up of his trays of fruits and vegetables to attend to a late shopper, and was silent for a few moments. As the light flashed amber and Gilly revved the engine she said, "I guess I can't feel tired because I'm buzzing so much with excitement; working with people like that in a project like this, thinking of all the people it will help."

"I have to say it was more of a laugh than I thought it would be. When are they hoping to get the ambulances all loaded up?" Gilly said.

"Well it's not absolutely fixed. As long as it takes, I guess. It's been running since the beginning of Ramadan on 26th May on weekdays so we don't get in the way of Tim's weekend services and groups. The plan is to be completely finished and ready for the convoy by 23rd June, the day before Eid celebrations begin."

In my head I counted the days. "So there are seven more days to get the job done? Now I've finished sorting out Gilly's assignment for him I'm freed up, so I should be able to come and help out for the rest of the time."

"Me too. Provided Dylan's made a good job of it, I can put in my final assignment, thank God."

"Thank me, you mean."

Gilly told us he would have taken us for a meal that evening to demonstrate his appreciation, but Em had bought tickets to see a live music act by some friends of hers in town.

I was quick to suggest a compromise. "How about you buy us a takeaway on the way home, mate? That will be grand, I promised Freya I'd do the cooking because she's had such a long day, but now I really can't be bothered."

"Be glad to, and I'll cook you both a meal with Em at my place over the weekend. Do you mind if I drop you off and give you the money for the food? I'd better not keep Em waiting."

"Perfect, thanks. I don't get paid by the warehouse until Friday. Freya, what do you fancy? Omar's? Great, that's just around the corner from mine, Gilly."

When we had unpacked the various silver trays from the paper bags, arranged them on the coffee table, grabbed spoons and bowls and peeled off the lids in drooling anticipation, Freya and I settled on the sofa ready to dive in to our feast. I lifted up the remote control to point it at the television. Freya gave the hand holding the gadget a soft tap with her spoon.

"Let's talk for a bit first. I've been dying to get you on my own for a while. I've so much to tell you, and I don't think I can wait any longer."

"Whoa, what's all this about?" I dipped a fat chip into my portion of mushroom curry and wiggled it around.

"Actually, on second thoughts I don't want to distract you from this lovely meal. There's going to be a lot to take in and it'll be best to do it on a full stomach. Besides, it's too good to let it go cold. So let's scoff first and discuss things later."

"Well, I'm way too hungry to argue with that. Does that mean I can put the telly on, mysterious girl?"

"As long as it's not the News please."

We continued eating; most of our attention on the food, a little of it on the quips of a comedy quiz show.

"Come on Freya, spit it out now," I said, mopping up

my aloo sag with a piece of naan bread.

She laughed, trying to keep her mouth full of onion bhaji closed, coughed, chewed and swallowed. "Well, are you ready for this? Jamal showed up this morning before her shift at the hospital, and was showing me her photographs and videos of the children in the refugee camps she has visited."

"Atif's sister? The doctor?"

"Yes, you met her when we presented the cheque from the Cycle Race to the Charity. Remember?"

"I think so. Where were the refugee camps? In Syria?"

"One on the Syrian border, one on the Turkish border. This will be the sixth convoy she has been with. This time she'll be travelling with Saffi. Now that Saffi is more confident, and she's had time to practice with her father's van, they'll be sharing the driving."

"Saffi is driving too?"

"Sure, and why shouldn't they be up to it as much as the men? Jamal says that since her first trip it's impossible for her to stay away. She's totally driven to help the poor people, and now Saffi feels the same. And guess what?"

I felt I had already guessed what. "What?"

"Each day I spend volunteering at the church, listening to the stories and seeing the pictures of the guys who've gone before, I've been thinking about it more and more. Until lately I can't stop thinking about it and I've been desperate to travel with them. So today when I was with Saffi and Jamal I plucked up the courage to ask if there was any chance that I could go with them."

"So what did they say?"

My chest swelled with love and admiration for my girlfriend, and constricted in concern for what she might be about to embark on.

"I think at first they were surprised, but also touched and excited. Jamal asked me if I was sure and if I'd thought very carefully and seriously about what was involved. I said I had, and she said that she would need some time to see what Atif and the others felt about it. When she left for the hospital Saffi was on pins, praying that I'd be allowed to travel with them."

"So you still don't know whether you can go or not?"

Again I was ambivalent, feeling a sense of relief mixed with disappointment and hope for Freya.

"Yes. No. This is the thing: Jamal had obviously had a word with Atif who must've had a chat with the others. They have a lot of respect for Jamal and Atif. I think as soon as it was clear that those two approved, the others were willing to go along with it. Just before you and Gilly arrived, I had a text from Jamal telling me they would be honoured and delighted to have me accompany them."

"Why didn't you tell me when I got to the church?"

"Well, I really wanted to tell you privately because I wasn't sure how you'd feel about it, and I wanted us to have the chance to discuss it first."

"I'm really happy for you if you want to do it that much. I can't say I blame you. I really get why you want to go but I'd be lying if I told you I had no worries."

Freya twisted round to wrap her arms round my neck and kissed my forehead.

"Bless you. I love you for that, Dyl, and I want you to know I've given it tons of thought from all angles. It's just something I really feel I've got to do, and there's no time better to do it than now after finishing uni. Before we have to get real jobs and all that crap."

"Yes, I'm not saying you don't know what you're doing or anything like that, but isn't it really dodgy going into Syria with the war going on?"

"Ah, see, here's the thing. Jamal is going to drive into Syria to deliver the aid to hospitals, schools and some centres, and remember she's done this five times before. Saffi and I are going to stay at the refugee camp on the Turkish side for the whole day. We'll help out there while the others complete the mission inside Syria. I asked Jamal about safety, and she says that takes personal precautions such as wearing a burka. Also they have a really reliable network of contacts they're in regular communication with, who know the area, liaise with medical staff, aid workers and even the armed groups."

"So, wow! And how do you think you'll fit in? I mean, I've never heard of a non-Muslim going with these convoys."

"Dylan! I'll fit in just as happily and comfortably as I always fit in with good friends, which is definitely what Saffi is, and I'm sure Jamal is going to become."

"Yeah, sorry, I didn't mean it that way. I guess I was thinking more about the others. The guys. Do you think they are really comfortable about you going?"

"Well, apart from not really having that much to do with them once the journey has begun, I imagine, we are all doing this in the same spirit. We all share the same motivation to help the ordinary people suffering from this dragged-out war. That's the important thing. It's what the InterFaith project is all about; shared values and all that."

"You're right. And you're amazing. Come here." I pulled her to me and stroked her hair; her breath warm on my chest. "Just be safe, that's all."

By the time I had carried out the empty bags, trays, bowls and cutlery, dumped the waste and washed up, Freya had dropped into a deep slumber on the sofa. Her arm dangled down the side, still holding her phone, which she had been using to show me the images and recordings Jamal had shared with her from the refugee camps. I eased the phone from her hand and placed it on the coffee table, before lifting her arm to return it to the other in a comfortable cradle.

From my modern, flimsy, bargain store desk I picked up my laptop and took it to the armchair adjacent to the sofa. When I opened up Talkbook the first thing I saw was a notification that Atif had tagged me, Freya, Gilly and some of the others in photographs taken at the church this afternoon. I accepted the tag on my Timeline Review and spent a few moments recalling the satisfaction of the work and the pleasure of our interaction. Atif and Saffi were already my Talkbook friends, and I noticed Mo and Naz, who I'd got to know better, had sent me friend requests which I confirmed. I wondered whether to add Jamal as a friend too, but I sensed reserve under her friendly manner which I put down to her being a medical doctor, although I had no idea if I was right. I found myself scrolling through the timelines of Atif, Mo and Naz, without knowing what my motivation was. Their posts shared similarities; excitement about recording the progress of the InterFaith project and evidence of the efforts of the volunteers, the contributors and the camaraderie. They all showed varying degrees of enjoyment of eating out and holidaying with friends, concern about the plight of Palestinians and love for sport and music. With an unpleasant sensation of snooping which I'd experienced before, though it did not stop me once I started, I clicked on the Friends list of Atif and begin looking through the names and profile pictures. I disliked that I was doing it but I knew who I was looking for. Scanning the five hundred friends of Atif was increasingly boring and time-consuming, and as I reached the end of the list I had still not found Saif. I was halfway through the even longer list of Mo's followers before I asked myself why I was doing it. Why was I feeling the compulsion to find out more about a guy who did not even seem to wish to be introduced to me earlier?

Saif's name came up in conversation on Saturday night, when Freya and I were having dinner at Gilly's place with Em, Ash and Ro, during our enthusiastic and detailed description of the InterFaith project.

"And do you know the latest?" Gilly said to the others. "Dylan and Freya are actually going to travel with them."

Ash and Ro stopped eating to look at each other with astonishment, their forks wound with spaghetti suspended like bobbins in mid-air. Ro spoke first. "You mean you're actually going to drive into Syria?"

"I'm only going as far as the Turkish border with Saffi," Freya said. "We're going to stay and help out at the refugee camp until the drivers come back. Only ten of the group will actually take the aid into Syria with workers on the ground, who will drive them back to the border because they're going to keep the ambulances."

"Wow." Ro puffed out of the side of his mouth at the little flop of hair above his left eye. "This has elevated quickly. How are you getting back if you're going to give away the ambulances once you get there?"

"I found us some cheap tickets from Antalya airport for 7th July, which is good, but we'll probably have to catch a coach or bus to get there. We'll have to see if the others have sorted that part out, as most of us are flying back from Antalya as far as I know." Freya looked to me. "Have you heard any more about that from Atif?"

I shook my head.

"I'll call him tomorrow. We've got a planning meeting booked for the 27th, two days before we leave, to look at the routes, schedule, all that kind of thing. It's all very well organised."

"How about you, Dylan? Don't tell me you're going in," Ash said. "That's wild, man."

"Not sure, to be honest. I volunteered for the convoy when Atif told me they were a driver short, and I said I'd like to see it through to the end. But he won't give me a definite yes at the moment. Half of our drivers will stay behind in the refugee camp at the Turkish border. The other half will hook up with people on the ground to take the stuff to the final destinations; the hospitals, schools, centres and wherever, because they're used to the territory and the conditions can be dangerous."

"Aren't they brave?" Em, who was seated between me and Gilly, slapped my shoulder, causing me to cough out some of my Bolognese sauce into my glass of beer.

"I wouldn't mind going myself on the big adventure,"

Gilly said. "But there's going to be a lot of long, hard driving, not to mention hardly any proper food to eat and sleeping rough in the ambulance. I mean, you're not really going to be able to get a shower or anything like that are you?"

"Well, we'll be stopping off at service stations and it's only for just over a week. Some things about it make me nervous to be honest, but mostly I'm really buzzing about it. And so is Freya."

Em raised her wineglass.

"It's totally exciting I have to say, though it does sound a bit scary too. But, as you say, those guys have been before and I'm sure they all know what they're doing, and who they're dealing with. The important thing is that those people get some help."

We all showed our agreement with Em's sentiment by chinking our drinks with hers.

"Does anyone want more wine, beer, coffee even?" As nobody wanted coffee, Em got up to get more bottles from the fridge. "All this talk of travelling to the Turkish border is making me think of my grandmother and other relatives because their village is only about fifty miles from the border. I really want to visit myself one day," she said.

The following morning I woke up late after a long lie-in, to a sunny day glowing behind the curtains. I congratulated myself for not feeling too bad at all after the boozy dinner at Gilly's, even though I succumbed to a sneaky smoke at one point. I decided to do a Skype call with Grandad for our usual Sunday catch-up, before Freya showed up with the eggs and bacon.

He answered quickly, and I eased myself into the conversation by listening to his comical observations about his week, his mixed bag of friends, his neighbours, his cat, my mother and other members of our family. When it came to my turn, I was pondering how to frame my forthcoming trip with the convoy to him. When I explained my plans he frowned and said nothing for several seconds, and I could feel myself sinking. At last he breathed in and nodded.

"Well, that's excellent work you'll be doing, son. With very good people I'm sure. You make me proud, Dylan, you know that. It's just that, being your old daft Grandad, I worry a bit and want to be sure you'll be safe."

"Don't worry about that Grandad. These guys are very experienced and most of them have been on several trips before. They've got good people on the ground over there too. I'd really like you to meet Atif and Saffi, I think you'd really like them.

"I'm sure I would, I'm sure I would. Just you and that lovely girl of yours look after yourselves, okay? Now you'd better tell your sister the craic. She's been hopping about in the background, dying to talk to you."

"Hi Dol. How's it going?"

"Oh, we are all grand. Same old, same old. But I've been listening here to what you've been telling Grandad. Are you telling me that my little brother who only got his driving licence last year, is going to drive an actual ambulance all the way to Syria?"

"Exactly that, Sis. Deal with it. Anyway, I'm going to be able to practice before we set off."

I could hear Grandad chuckling with us in the background.

"Thank Jesus for that. I don't think I could drive an ambulance to save my life."

Chapter 4

Atif was good enough to show me the ropes, when I could get the time between my packing job at the warehouse and helping out with the packing and loading at Carmel Church. My manager had been very decent about letting me have the ten days off to travel with the convoy at such short notice, which included a day either side to prepare and rest up a bit. For no good reason I felt guilty because I intended to pack it in as soon as something better came along. After all, it was only ever meant to be a part-time job to help me get through university without being completely skint all the time.

"Dylan. I've got some good news for you. At least I hope you think so." Atif fastened his seatbelt in the passenger seat, looking very cheerful and more importantly, calm, as we set off on our first run with me in the driver's seat of the ambulance.

"What's that then?" I said, pressing my index finger and palm on the keys, waiting to turn on the ignition.

"I've been talking to the guys, and they agreed to a bit of a reshuffle of the main drivers and co-drivers." He explained to me that each ambulance was to have a designated main driver, the most experienced, who would be responsible for delivering the aid and the ambulance inside Syria. The co-drivers were to remain behind the Turkish border. "So Mo has agreed to swap and travel with Abdullah so that you and I can team up. As we're pretty good friends already, the guys and I thought you be more comfortable with me."

"Fantastic. Yes, thanks mate. You know I'm really excited about this trip anyway, and this makes it even better. I take it you're going to be the main driver?"

"No bro. You're going to be the main man. What else did you think?"

"Right." I took my hand off the keys because we were laughing too much, and there were a couple of questions I wanted to get off my mind before I really put my attention to getting on the road. "Okay, but joking aside, I was kind of hoping I'd get to go the whole hog, complete the mission sort of thing."

"Well it is a bit of a 'names out of the hat' kind of process. But in your case, because it's your first time and whatever, you probably won't like to hear this but you were left out of the equation."

"So who is paired up with who?"

"I'll start with the names of the main drivers first: you know Jamal will be with Saffi and Freya, Mo and Abdullah, Naz and Hani, Rajwan with Talal."

I interrupted him with the name that was foremost in my mind, for reasons I did not understand or want to examine.

"What about Saif?"

Either Atif did not think it was a strange question or he didn't want to know why I was asking it. "Hang on, I've not finished yet. Saif is taking the place of Abdullah so he'll be with Zaheel."

"Okay. I doubt I'll remember all the combinations or even everybody's names right now. Shall we get going?"

"Yep, let's hit the road bro. First, it might be a good idea to get a feel for this beast in the car park, especially as it's pretty empty right now."

Atif has the patience of a saint. He did not flinch at my clunky braking or changing gears, my tendency to speed up when other vehicles instinctively slowed down as they saw us coming, or my clumsy taking of corners.

"You're doing great, you're doing great. You're getting it fine bro. Just remember it's quite a bit heavier than what you're used to driving. And Dylan, do me a favour. Get it into your head that you're not a real ambulance."

His calmness and encouragement helped me to get the hang of it and settle from an excited edginess into concentration. By the time we had driven out of town into the more rural roads, I was ready to take on the motorway route back to suburbia.

"Good job Dylan," Atif said, as I handed him back the keys. "Nice parking too. Not bad for a first run."

Minister Tim jogged over to us from across the hall, flapping his hands, his cartoon smile heralding good news. He reached us just as we flopped down beside Freya and Saffi who were sitting on pallets of baby food.

"Just the young men I want to see. I don't suppose these wonderful young ladies have told you about our plans for a little celebration?"

"Sounds good," Atif said, "I'm always up for a celebration."

Tim crossed his palms over his heart, looked up, closed his eyes and beamed. We waited until he opened his eyes and arms.

"Janet and I thought it would be a good idea to hold a little party on the third day of Eid, 26th of June, because not only would that be a very good day to do so, it will be an opportunity to get together all the volunteers to show appreciation for all the good work, and also as a kind of blessing to send off the convoy on the 29th."

We looked at each other, making approving noises. "That is such a good idea, Tim," Freya said, "how are you thinking of organising it?"

"Janet suggested a Jacob's Joint for the food and we will provide all the drinks. Janet thinks a little wine and beer would be perfectly appropriate, don't you agree? We can have it here in the hall which is going to be clear by the beginning of Eid anyway, so we thought early evening, about six?"

"Great," I said, "but what's a Jacob's Joint?"

They all began to explain to me at the same time, then laughed and allowed Saffi to enlighten me.

"It's when everyone brings a different dish of their own. It can be anything. Savoury, sweet, spicy, salads, desserts, nibbles. You get the idea?"

"The idea sounds great," I said, "but does it all have to

be home-made?"

Freya nudged me. "Don't worry Dylan, we'll put our name down for the sweet stuff, okay? Because we're not going to embarrass ourselves by bringing anything from the supermarket, and trust me, the spicy department is best left to the masters here." She indicated Atif and Saffi with an open hand. "And other friends, including Janet of course."

Tim looked gratified for the mention of his wife.

Freya told me more about what a Jacob's Joint entailed on the drive home to my place. Her description left me salivating because of the afternoon's graft, the hour in the ambulance that had strained my nerves and my mind, and the details of all the wonderful, diverse and aromatic dishes she anticipated the other guests would bring.

"So you said you'd do a sweet. Are you thinking of a dessert, a cake or something like that?"

"Less competition there. Don't want to show myself up." Freya laughed and licked her lips. "It's going to be so good. I can manage a trifle, possibly cheesecake or a lemon drizzle cake. Something. You could throw a salad together, couldn't you?"

"What about something traditionally Irish?"

"Potatoes in many forms? Maybe you can come up with something interesting."

"Maybe. But please, let's just stop talking about food. I'm literally starving."

"So guys, what you think of this?" Ro said on Saturday evening, the day after my first ambulance driving experience.

We were about to begin guzzling our tapas in Jenny and Alfie's trendy bar in the main street of the hip neighbourhood of South Mancaster, not far from Ash's apartment in a converted old convent.

"You're not the only ones who've been planning adventures. Ash and I were talking about you going to

Turkey and we've been thinking of taking a holiday there for ages. Ash has booked the first two weeks in July off already, to get away before the schools' summer holidays start, and of course we've got to be back by the third week for our Graduation do. We've found a beautiful villa, sleeps six, in a peaceful little place by the beach east of Antalya."

"And? Gilly winked. "Sounds very lovely but there seems to be an 'and' to it. Am I right?"

"Yes you're right, as always. Sarcasm aside, we've booked it for a really good price for two weeks from Sunday, 2nd July, and were hoping that you guys would like to join us."

"Sounds like a plan." Gilly looked at Em for confirmation. "Amazing. A couple of weeks chilling in the sun should set us up nicely to look our best for the Graduation photos. Book me in guys. I'll start looking for flights in the morning. How about you Em? You don't have anything else on do you?"

"Hey, if I did I'd dump it for a couple of weeks in Turkey. Maybe I'll be able to fit in a little trip to see my grandmother and my family in the East. That would be so exciting."

"Cool. Do it." Freya was checking her calendar on her phone. "You know the convoy leaves on the 29th, so Dylan and I should be free around the 6th. We were flying back from Antalya anyway, so I can't see any problem changing our flight times."

"There you go. That's why we booked it from 2nd July, so you could join us for a well-earned break seeing as you're going to be in the country anyway," Ash said.

"God, you guys are the best," said Freya. "Isn't that right Dylan?"

"It sounds so tempting. It would be perfect just to hang out on the beach with our gang, after we've delivered the ambulances and all the aid. I'm sure we could use some downtime after that."

"So what's stopping you?" said Ro. "It's the ideal time to get away together and celebrate finishing uni, before we have to start hunting those pay cheques. We can all relax and contemplate our grown-up futures. Or not. The time of our lives."

"Let's not talk about becoming slaves for now. I'm still dreaming of a freer future. The holiday's a fantastic idea and really generous of you two, but I'm not sure I'll be able to swing it with work. Once I've taken the ten days annual leave for the convoy trip, I think I'll only have a couple of days due to me."

"You can always throw a sickie," Gilly said. "You can call them from Turkey and tell them you've developed some horrific stomach complaint in the refugee camp. You'll get a lot of sympathy points for that as well."

"Haha. Thanks for your advice Gilly, but I prefer to ask first."

"Or maybe we can just kidnap you?"

"Funny that. Are you just trying to distract me from the fact that you're hogging the mushrooms? Pass them over Frey. Please. Shall we order some more tortillas, and wine come to think of it? I might go for the Italian draught lager."

As it happened I could not swing it. My line manager, Ben, had been very supportive of my initial request. When I asked him for an extra ten days unpaid holiday leave, he sucked his yellowed teeth and told me he would have to take my application higher. He went off to talk to his boss. It took him forty-five minutes to call me back to his office from my workstation. "Sorry Dylan, the boss thinks you're taking the Mick now. He says no way, mate."

I don't know if I'll ever know exactly what possessed me. There seemed to be an urgent, quiet whisper inside me, not just in my head but in every cell in my body; persistent and repetitive. It led me to say, "In that case I might as well hand in my notice now. I'm not coming back."

Chapter 5

Reflecting on my impulsiveness when I had finished the Monday morning shift, I ruminated over a hoisin duck wrap in my car before driving over to Carmel Church. I began to wonder whether I should have just thrown the towel in there and then. My excitement at the prospect of the convoy setting off in just ten days was being drained by the overwhelming realisation of all that had to be done and was left to do. To be fair, I thought, the Boss did have a point about me expecting to be able to disappear for three weeks at the drop of a hat. At least I'd get another week's pay and a fortnight's paid leave. Seven more six-hour shifts and I would be done. The eager anticipation of that ending pushed out my fear of not having enough money to survive on. I had a sense of rightness about my decisions and that anything could happen, anyway. In the meantime there was still a lot to be accomplished at the church, the loading of the ambulances, and the stuff I had to do to be ready for both the mission and the holiday afterwards. I still hadn't found my passport, but at least Atif said all the other paperwork for the journey would be taken care of by the date of our departure.

There were just five days to complete the task of loading the supplies before our deadline of Friday, June 24th, the day before Eid. My shifts at the warehouse that week were all in the morning; from eight until two in the afternoon, so by the time I had grabbed something to eat and drink and got over to the church, I could only offer a few hours of help. Atif, who looked paler and more exhausted as the days went on, must have been desperate to get home, when instead he made time to go out in the ambulance for my driving practice, and never showed me anything but support.

"You're doing great, bro. I mean it, and anyway you'll have plenty of time to find your feet once we're on the road. Those European motorways are long, long, long I tell you." He smiled when I told him about handing my notice in at the warehouse. "No kidding?"

"I know. I surprised myself. It just came out of my mouth and it felt like the right thing to do."

"Well, I'll trust you on that. I do know one thing though, that travelling with these aid convoys can start to feel like an addiction."

I thought of telling him about my sense of purpose and mission, which I knew he would understand, and how the idea of going to Syria felt as if it had overtaken every cell in my body. I stopped myself because I didn't want to hear him say that I was going to be left behind at the border. I wanted to see it through to the end so much.

As I left the warehouse behind me on Friday afternoon, knowing that this was the last day to get the vehicles ready to go I was firing on adrenaline. I received another shot of happiness when I saw Gilly pulling up in his car outside the church with Em in the passenger seat. Perhaps Freya had called them to say we needed all the help we could get today. The look on Atif's and the other volunteers' faces when they saw them walking through the door with me mirrored my gratitude.

Atif leapt over, grabbed Gilly's hand and upper arm and beamed at Em.

"Thanks so much for coming, guys. You don't know how much we appreciate this. I'm beginning to think we might have to carry on working until about eight or even nine, Dylan, so there's no way we're going to get out in the ambulance later.

"No worries. Let's get the most important job done."

All the drivers were loading up their own vehicles with the help of a few volunteers who were not taking part in the actual journey. Gilly teamed up with Atif and me, loading up the medical supplies we would be taking. This was also the cargo of Jamal, Saffi and Freya, whom Em began to help. We had been working for about thirty minutes when Gilly looked up, shouted and pointed at the door.

"Sweet. You made it." We began to clap as Ro and Ash walked towards us. "The cavalry has arrived." Gilly introduced them to the welcoming cluster in our part of the hall. "Really appreciate this," he said, putting his arm around Ash's shoulder. "Especially you, mate, as I know it's your precious day off from serving and protecting us peasants."

Ash answered with a modest laugh while we guffawed.

"Don't mention it. Happy to help." He looked around the hall at the various stacks and stacks and the people bundling them. "Where do you want us?"

Atif beckoned Naz, who put down the tower of boxes in his arms and strolled over.

"We've got extra hands, Naz. Could you use some help over there?"

Naz shook the hands of Ash and Ro. "Good to meet you. Thanks for helping us out." He took a step back and looked more closely at Ash's face. "Have I met you before? I feel as if I know your face from somewhere."

Ash looked as if he was trying to recall some previous encounter.

"Not sure. Where do you live?"

"South side. I've got it now. I think I met you in a youth club about five years ago. Did you used to be a cop?"

Ash laughed as he matched the recollection.

"That's going back a bit, seems like a long time ago now. Yeah, it must be when I first started out in the Police Force. Complete rookie. I wasn't giving you a hard time was I?"

"No, you were cool. I think you just dropped in with your good-looking copess to have a chat, get to know us a bit."

"Ha ha, good times. It's all coming back to me now."

"So, are you still with the boys in blue or what?"

"I am, only I moved over to the CID a couple of years

ago. How about you, as I guess you're not technically a youth any more?"

"CID eh? Even cooler. I'm training to be a dentist."

"I might have sussed that out," Ash said, pointing at Naz's smile. "Nice teeth man."

Naz led him and Ro away, one hand on each of their backs, laughing.

The progress with the packing was accelerated by the assistance of eight pairs of fresh, enthusiastic hands. By five o'clock we were reassured by the likelihood that we had little more than an hour's work to complete our tasks, and lock up the ambulances with their precious loads inside. That expectation energised us all, especially the steadfast Muslim volunteers whose anticipation of feasting buzzed through the hall.

Freya was satisfied enough that we were on track to whisper to me that she really needed to have a little snack and get some air, so she was going to take five minutes out. "Hang on a sec. I'll come with you."

Outside, away from the dust of dried foodstuff and cardboard, the air felt clean, clear and refreshing, and the sunlight was warming and welcome after the cool dimness of the church hall. We crossed over the road to the little community garden opposite, and sat down to break off pieces of the flapjack Freya produced from her bag, taking discreet nibbles and turns to share the water bottle with our backs turned to the church.

It made us both jump to hear a loud voice shouting from the other side of the street: "So that's where you are." Gilly clearly found it hilarious to see how much he'd startled us. "What are you doing over here?"

"We could ask you the same question," I said. "We're just taking a little break and having a bite to eat. How about you?"

"I need a smoke. So why didn't you just sit out in the church courtyard?"

Freya brushed some oats off her chin and top with her

fingers. "We just feel guilty eating in front of the ones who are fasting, that's all."

"Oh, that Catholic thing."

"What do you mean?" said Freya, offering Gilly the last slice of flapjack in the tray.

"Guilt. Catholic guilt. No thanks, this will take the edge off feeling hungry. You want me to roll up one for you as well, Dylan?"

Gilly sat down on our bench and began sprinkling tobacco leaves into the delicate cigarette paper curved between his fingers, placing the tip and expertly rolling it between his fingers. The rich, not quite sweet, aroma of the leaves reached my nose, enticing me. As usual, although I had never officially started smoking, I couldn't resist and nodded in collusion with him. These days Gilly pretended to have given up smoking too.

Freya reached out for a drag before my delicious moments of vice were over. I threw my dimp on the ground to crush it with my boot, picked it up when it was dead and took it over to the bin at the entrance to the garden. I noticed someone coming through the church doors. I called out to him: "Saif, are you off now? Eid Mubarak. Have a great weekend."

Saif glanced over his right shoulder at me and held up the back of his hand in acknowledgement, as he strode away from us without a word.

"Where did he come from? I didn't notice him inside the church before," Freya said, watching him disappear around the corner of a row of terraced houses. "He's a bit of a mystery, I have to say. My impression is it's not just me who thinks that. Nobody seems to know him very well, not even the other guys, I mean not in the way they are with each other. He never seems to take part in the banter either."

"Dark horse," said Gilly.

Chapter 6

A brutal, blinding tidal wave of light woke me up as Freya flung back the bedroom curtains on Saturday morning. Lining my palms up with my temples to make blinkers so I could look at what she was waving in front of my nose, I focused on the narrow notepad she used to make her 'to do' lists. "Dylan, we're going to have to get going if we're to get everything done. I've got myself into a right old panic this morning. I've realised we're leaving in five days. Five days!"

"Okay, okay, I'm waking up. Just let me get some coffee and let's have breakfast before we sit down and think about what needs to be done."

"Right, I'll put the kettle on. But how about you grab coffee and a shower, then we can set off, have breakfast in town and make a list while we're waiting for it?"

"Good idea, let's do that. Only I'm thinking that the first thing I should do before anything else is find my passport. I don't even know where it is at the moment."

"No? Dylan, what are you like?"

"Don't worry, I'll find it."

"Why don't you ever put things away in a fixed place so you know where they are? When was the last time you used it?"

"Well, with me not exactly being a seasoned traveler...that would have to be when we went to Amsterdam at Easter in the second year of uni."

"Last year then? So do you still have the rucksack you took with you? Could it be in there?"

"Genius. I do." I wagged a finger towards the bottom of my wardrobe, where out of the open doors a pair of crumpled jeans was crawling onto the floor. "Do me a favour, Lovely, just see if it's in there, maybe where the shoes are supposed to go."

My rucksack hit me on the side of the head as I turned to snuggle back under the duvet. The consolation was that the zipped pocket on the side that hit me had weight in it, which turned out to be my missing passport. "Yay," I said, waving it in the air. "What a relief. Thanks, well done."

"You're welcome, my love. Now just get your sorry ass in gear. Please."

The drive into Mancaster, which could take as little as twenty minutes on a good day if the timing was right, promised to be three times longer and more tedious, as the columns of cars slowed down and stacked on the motorway. We decided to hedge our frustration by verbally itemising the things we needed to have and do. Freya cheered up at the thought of planning and making lists.

"We should start with the basics I think. Like sleeping bags and pillows. We've both got them. Atif and Jamal have basic cooking equipment, so we should be okay for brewing tea and coffee, cooking eggs and some simple stuff. We can take things like cereal, oat and rice cakes, things like that. I'm hoping we'll be able to get fresh milk, bread, fruit and vegetables and cheese on the way, like we did when we got the Eurostar to France."

"What about pot noodles?" I said to annoy her.

She didn't answer but instead gave me a dismissive huff and a slap on my knee. I liked the amusement.

"I'm really looking forward to being able to sample some of the local-grown produce, so I hope we'll be able to be able to stop now and then to do that."

"Like cheese and wine?" I exaggerated smacking my lips to entertain myself as well as her. The traffic was at a standstill.

Freya mimicked me. "Definitely cheese and wine."

"Wait a minute, do you think the others will mind us drinking wine?"

" I'm pretty sure Atif and Saffi won't, so I'd be surprised if Jamal was bothered. If the others do we will just have to sneak off on our own like naughty teenagers."

"I like the sound of that." I pressed the gas pedal with my foot to rev the engine as the car in front of me eased forward.

"Anyway, we're getting distracted. I think I've got enough of the right clothes to take on the convoy; T-shirts, jeans, trainers and sweatshirts should do it, comfortable stuff and something warm in case it gets cool at night."

"Same. But I will need some things for the beach holiday, a beach towel, beach shorts and flip-flops. Ah, it feels good just to talk about it. Sunglasses, remind me to get sunglasses, a decent pair. I'll really need those. You thinking of packing the beach things in a separate bag?"

"I am, I think that will be best. Suncream, we need to put that on the list."

By the time we'd got to Mancaster and parked up we went for lunch rather than breakfast. Freya was quiet while we waited for our paninis and coffees, busy with her pen and paper, scribbling down the items we had thought of on the way. "Another thing I wanted to do is find some Eid gifts for Atif and Saffi, and maybe something like chocolates for the others, to give them on Monday at the Jacob's Joint party," she said.

"Nice. Any ideas?"

"Mmm, it's hard to know what to get. I was thinking of smellies. You know, maybe perfume and aftershave, that sort of thing."

"That could be tricky. How do you know what they like?"

"Easy for Saffi, because I know what she likes and what she uses. As for Atif, I'll have to use my nose and my memory. He usually smells pretty good, not like some people I know." Freya wrinkled her nose and laughed.

"Er, I hope you're not referring to the most wonderful man in your life?"

"Ach, you're not so bad most of the time, except when you're wafting in from the warehouse."

"Thanks. Ashes of Dustbins my Grandma used to say. It was one of her favourite jokes."

"Ashes of dustbins?"

"Yeah, because some popular cheap perfumes in her day were given names like Ashes of Roses."

"Ha ha, lovely. Well, I think we can do better than that, especially if you go halves with me. Enough nattering. Shall we make a move?"

The highlight of the afternoon for me was finding a solar charger for my phone and laptop. I hate shopping at the best of times. Especially in city centres on Saturday afternoons in crowded department stores full of poor quality crap: mass-produced by cheap labour in conditions you don't even want to get me started talking about. It was in such a place we ended our expedition, when Freya had bought two bargain bikinis and three dark, plain headscarves which she explained to me were, "For Turkey," then added, "I mean the bikinis are for afterwards at the beach, and the headscarves are for before, if you get what I mean."

"I think so. You'll look beautiful in both. Are we done now? I really want to get home and chill." I received a kiss on my chin for the compliment, and her agreement.

"If we can get everything ready for the trip tomorrow, we can relax a bit on Monday. We'll just have to prepare the food and wrap the presents to the church party then."

The heavens opened on Monday morning which gave me an excuse to delay the shopping Freya had asked me to do, and linger in bed for an hour longer until the battering of rain died down. I was peeling a banana to slice over my muesli, a habit new enough to give me a mild sense of virtue, when Freya walked into the kitchen. "I was thinking of cooking a full Irish breakfast at lunchtime after we get organised with the food. If we fill our boots early on it'll keep us going until the evening, then we should have a good appetite for the buffet. I want to have room in my belly for everything."

"Gannet." I gave her a playful prod in the stomach with my spoon. "Don't worry, I can manage a full Irish any time. Have you got the list for me for the shops?"

"Bully. Yes, I have a list of course, darling, including the stuff for your potato salad. Do you have any Guinness in?"

"Strange request, but no. Why Guinness? You're not thinking of drinking it with your breakfast, are you?"

"I certainly am. Do you want to join me?" Joining in her laughter caused me to sputter out some soggy oat flakes and almond chips. "Eww," she said, mopping her neck with a tea towel. "Don't be daft, I thought I'd better keep the side up, seeing as you're throwing in some tatties. I've decided to make a Guinness Chocolate Cake as well as some Barm Brack for tonight."

"Bit alcoholic eh? When my Gran made Barm Brack she used to soak the raisins in whiskey first."

"Did she now? No, I'm not going as far as that. Now it's stopped raining will you go and get the ingredients when you've finished that?"

"Bully."

Even if the contents of my big fry-up had not metabolised by the time we arrived at the church just after six, I still would not have been able to resist the food. A sensory rainbow of textures and aromas was arranged in dishes, bowls, platters and boards on the trestle tables covered in white cloth along one side of the hall. Minister Tim, with his specs, sparse feathers of salt-and-pepper hair, bright orange shirt and dog collar, stood behind the table in the centre. His arms were out-stretched, palms open in appreciation of the delicious display of divine abundance before him. Beaming volunteers flanked him, moving food around to make room for more, placing serving spoons and other utensils, inviting the guests to begin the feast. Though Tim bore no resemblance to Jesus, the scene reminded me of a modern artist's take on 'The Last Supper.' Perhaps 'The Last Buffet' was more fitting?

Amongst the neat arrows of cheese and tuna sandwiches lying on beds of lettuce, with bits of tomato and cucumber peeping out like eyes, were glistening salads and sauces, chunky and smooth. Crispy Chinese dumplings, with soft secret centres of subtly spiced prawn and duck, cosied up to chicken drumsticks red-hot with peppers, delicate sushi, kebabs, pakoras, and bhajis. Breadsticks and carrot and celery crudités stood in glass tumblers, ready to dunk in creamy and tangy dips. At the opposite end of the table to the paper plates, napkins and plastic cutlery were the sweets; fruit, nuts, dates, figs, a cheeseboard, some cakes and desserts I recognised, and exotic ones I didn't and couldn't wait to try. Freya's Barm Brack and Guinness Chocolate Cake were conversation starters, especially the cake which got mixed reactions, most of them quite humourous.

The thirteen year-old daughter of Tim and Janet was a shy girl with a pretty almond face, luminous, golden-brown skin, big, round blue eyes and cinnamon coloured, long Afro hair that rippled like grasses in a tropical breeze. She appeared to have been put in charge of the music and to be embarrassed by her job. I suspected that was because the hybrid music of Cat Stevens, who is now also known as Yusuf, was mostly easy to listen to but difficult to dance to. Although Sally was the D.J. her mother seemed to be directing the choice of music. After she had whispered in her daughter's ear, Yusuf was given a rest and replaced with the throbbing drum rhythms of African pop.

"Zulu," mouthed Janet as she strutted past me, her flesh wobbling with considerable musicality. Her head with its halo of hair, shorter, darker but otherwise similar to her daughter's, was bobbing like a bird's.

The music turned out to be as eclectic as the food. After a selection of the current Western Top Ten hits and some reggae, we were treated to Asian hip-hop that some of the guests had on their phones, which Sally played through a Bluetooth speaker she brought down from her bedroom. We party-goers, refreshed and primed for action by the food, and ready to take a break from conversation, became lively and expanded into the space.

At the end of the second track, I noticed the dancers stepping back to form an aisle for a fragile-looking but sprightly old lady, dressed in a shin-length, navy summer raincoat and a headscarf decorated with gold anchors knotted under her chin. She was holding up a rolled-up sheaf of paper like a torch, making her way towards Tim, who was near the stage, jerking happily out of the time to the beat. Her spare hand was covering her left ear, and her eyes were half closed as if in pain. Sally must have taken this as a sign to press the pause button on the speaker, because the room was silent when Tim noticed the visitor approaching.

"Mrs Piggott, how nice to see you. Have you come to join our little party?"

Mrs Piggott closed her eyes fully, with a slight shudder of her face and a short sniff of offence taken. "Oh no, no, no. Not at all. I'd forgotten you were having at do, and I'm really sorry to disturb you in the middle of it, Reverend."

"Tim."

"Well, Reverend Tim, I just needed to let you know that Penny is going to have her hip done on Friday. She got in on a cancellation and won't be able to play the organ on Sunday. Now Anne has said she is willing to do it but she's not familiar with all the hymns. So I've had to make some changes on the hymn sheet and let the choir know."

"I do hope Penny will be all right," said Tim, joining his hands. "Is there anything I can do to help?"

"No, nothing, I just thought I'd better let you know."

"Yes, thank you very much Mrs Piggott, you do seem to have everything in hand."

Janet squeezed through the gap between the choir mistress and the Minister, and put her arm around Mrs Piggott's shoulders.

"Are you sure you won't stay for a little bite to eat with us, Betty? The food is out of this world. And we're going to have a little toast in a few minutes, aren't we Tim, if you'd like to join us?"

Betty Piggott's expression grew tighter; a little panicked.

"No, I must go," she said with a rasp, fingering a gold cross at the well of her throat, looking round at us. We shifted our positions and began talking again amongst ourselves. Before the old lady had reached the exit we were startled by the sudden boom of rap starting up again. I presumed that Mrs P. had moved out of Sally's line of vision.

Later, I wondered if the two messengers had crossed paths at the door. No sooner had we begun to ease into our moves again when some dancers were separated by the more haphazard and urgent route of a familiar male figure in black. With his hood up and his hands hidden in his pockets, he strode towards Atif, alternately glaring at the speaker and giving curt responses to greetings from the guests he brushed by. Tim did not seem to notice the newcomer; he climbed up on the stage, rubbed his right knee and signalled to his daughter to turn off the music. He clapped his hands and waved at us.

"Friends, friends, if I may have your kind attention please. Thank you. Have no fear, the party has not yet come to an end, but before we proceed any further I should like to give a short speech and propose a toast in honour of and gratitude for our most kind and dedicated team of volunteers." He paused, pleased by the burst of applause. "My lovely wife is stationed over there, ready with the drinks. There is Prosecco and French beer as well as a range of soft drinks and sparkling water, so please do go over and get yourself a glass."

Atif, who was standing next to me in the drinks queue, looked over his shoulder to see who had placed a hand on it.

"Saif, good to see you. Glad you could make it, I thought you weren't coming."

I reached Janet's bar table and asked for a beer. Turning round I said, "Can I get you guys anything?"

Saif glanced down his long, fine nose at the bottle in my hand.

"Not for me, I'm not hanging around for long. There's just something important I need to tell Atif. He pulled my friend out of the line by his sleeve.

"Get me a Coke bro," Atif said as he was led away.

He returned just in time to raise it at the end of Tim's effusive speech of thanks to the givers and the workers, and wishes to the members of the convoy for a safe and blessed journey.

"What was all that about?" I said, repeating it louder because Sally had started up the hip-hop again.

"Come outside for a minute and I'll tell you before I let the others know." Atif scratched his head and wiped his face with his hand. "Have you got any baccy? Can you do me a roll-up? I'm feeling I need to process this a bit." In the church courtyard, he waited until I handed him the thin cigarette I had hand-rolled with Gilly's tobacco before he spoke. "Thanks. This is freaking me out a bit, which it probably shouldn't but it's such short notice, and none of us really know the guy."

"What guy?"

Atif took the lighter out of my hand and lit up.

"Right, sorry. You remember Zaheel, the friend of Saif's cousin? Well, Saif came to tell me that Zaheel has family problems so now he can't come with us, but he says he's got another brother, a family friend, to take the place of Zaheel. His name is Rafeed."

"So what did you say? I mean, is that going to be okay with us going in three days and all that?"

"It's going to have to be, innit?" Atif took a deep suck on his smoke, threw the cigarette end down and stamped on it.

"So why didn't Saif bring Rafeed with him tonight, to introduce him to everybody as soon as he could?"

"He said Rafeed was too busy to come as he has so much to do. Obviously. Apparently he's an optometrist in

Bradford so he'll have to move around his appointments in the next few days to prepare for the trip. Saif says he's going to join us for the planning meeting tomorrow so we'll get to meet him then, Inshallah."

The Weight Watchers regarded us with suspicious eyes as we intruded on their weigh-in; all twenty-two of us trooping through Camel Church hall twenty-four hours after our Jacobs Joint party had begun. Janet, who was navigating us through, spoke to their leader, a dour, plump woman in a trouser suit and high heels. In a voice loud enough for all to hear she explained who we were and what our purpose was, and the hostility subsided into smiles of approval. A few slimmers clapped.

The main topic of conversation, as we waited outside the Community Room for the Christian Meditation group to leave, was about how good the food the evening before had been. Freya concluded that her Guinness Chocolate Cake was like Marmite. Those who had been greedy or curious enough to taste it either loved it or hated it, from all accounts.

"I was tempted enough by the Guinness," I said, "but it's a pity I don't like chocolate cake."

When the smiling meditators had all left the room in friendly form we pushed four tables together to make a large square in the middle of the room, and placed chairs around it. As we were all getting seated, Atif placed a map and two sheets of paper in front of each of our positions.

"Hi brothers and sisters. Welcome to our planning meeting for the important and exciting humanitarian mission we are about to carry out. I'm going to start straightaway as we have a lot to cover and I know, if you're like me, you still have a lot to do before we set off on Thursday morning. We'll start with the introductions, because even though most of us already know each other we have a new member with us today."

We all looked towards the tiny man with stooped

shoulders sitting next to Saif. Our attention seemed to increase his shyness, which made him look smaller. He lowered his eyes behind his expensive-looking, iridescent glasses, stroking his neat, short, black beard, hiding his mouth with his fingers. Atif introduced him to the group.

"This is brother Rafeed who, as I explained to you last night, is at very short notice taking the place of Zaheel, who unfortunately cannot be with us due to personal family problems, which he says rightly it is his first duty to attend to. I'm sure you will join me in sending duas to Zaheel and his family, and saying thank you and welcome to his replacement, Rafeed." His announcement was followed with murmurs of support for the missing man and greetings to his substitute.

"Although all of you are meeting him for the first time," said Saif, "I can vouch for Rafeed who is a family friend. He's been recommended by Zaheel for his commitment and devotion to our humanitarian cause, and experience travelling with several convoys like ours."

Saif received our nods, smiles and comments of approval well. He relaxed and gave us a smile so broad it was the first time I had seen his superior teeth.

Atif began the meeting proper with what he called the basic rules; a kind of code of conduct, simple etiquette, and health and safety guidelines.

"Now we've got that out of the way, I'd like to discuss us taking on certain designated roles. Although I think it's understood that we'll all be working as a team, ready to chip in as, when and where we're needed, it's good to use peoples' strengths and expertise. So as we identify key people, I suggest you consider who you might partner up with in the most useful way. Is everyone okay with that?"

We were.

"Great. So as you all know, my role is general coordinator; I'll present the paperwork and do the talking when necessary, including in my rather inferior Arabic. Luckily, my dear sister Jamal is much more fluent than me and ready to help me out. So, we've pencilled in suggestions for some of the main roles which I'll go through. We've had informal chats about this before, but please stop me if you've got any questions or ideas. Speaking of my wonderful sister, as she is a medical doctor, predictably we are putting her in charge of first-aid, general health and well-being, perhaps with the aid of Naz and Rafeed because of their related professions? Mo is the obvious choice for vehicle maintenance as he is such a genius on that score, so maybe two or three of you will be ready to be his grease monkeys."

Atif gave us time to stop chattering, conferring and scribbling down notes.

"Before we talk about some other roles, I want to mention something that is related and needs to be considered before we go on. Those of you who've travelled with convoys before know how giving and supportive a lot of people in the different countries we travel to want to be. In the past, we have experienced amazing kindness from locals in the form of water, food, little luxuries and even money. Some of it we use for ourselves if it is helpful and makes our mission easier, some of it we save for the Syrian aid. That's usually not a problem, with the exception of money, which we have to be accountable for. We need to show what has come in and where it has gone out. With that in mind, as you are an actual accountant, would you be happy with that job, Saif?"

"More than happy."

"Good man, we'll find you a helper. Now, with regard to the distribution of food gifts, because you, Abdullah, are a wonderful, talented restaurateur, I can't pronounce that, will you be in charge of that side of things? Freya and Saffi have said they'll be glad to help you out with that. Now, before we sort out who else can be doing what else and all that, Dylan here has also suggested a special role doing something he's very good at."

My relief, that Atif had got round to mentioning what had been on my mind since we started, clashed with my nervousness about how the group would respond. It spiked when Atif asked me to explain. I told them about my background and how I would really like to record a photo and video journal of the trip.

"Obviously you will only be filmed if you really feel comfortable with it, and everyone will get the chance to have a say in what the content will be and also the final edit."

As I looked around at the faces to gauge their reaction I was excited by the enthusiasm they expressed, with the exception of Saif and Rafeed, who were looking down at their paperwork.

"There you go, Naz," Atif said, "you've always fancied yourself in the movies. Fantastic. Okay, let's quickly agree on the remaining roles and then we can have some fun with the maps."

We pored over the maps, tracing the route Mo described with our fingers, and checked the details of our schedule. I could feel the energy in the room thicken and quicken with the excitement leaking out from us, bonding us like glue, or so I imagined.

"So, the next time we will meet, brothers and sisters, will be at five-thirty in the morning this Thursday, less than two days. Friendly reminder that we intend to set off at six a.m. sharp, Inshallah, so take care and be on time."

With hugs or handshakes and some manic goodbyes, we parted, clutching our maps and plans.

When Freya and I had settled on the settee in front of the television, she with a glass of wine, me with a beer, I found myself scrolling through Talkbook in search of Saif again, and also this time his partner Rafeed. It took me an hour to find Rafeed first, and he in turn led me to Saif. As I was not an official Friend there was not much I could view, although what I did see surprised me. Neither of the pair were Talkbook friends with any of the other drivers of the convoy, except Zaheel who was no longer part of it. Unlike the profiles of the other drivers there were few images of a personal nature, and the titles they both gave under their profile pictures were identical: 'Humanitarian Aid Worker.' One post by Rafeed, which was on a public setting rather than a private one, Saif and others unknown to me had liked and commented on. It was written in Arabic, which Google translated for me as "Please give duas for our brothers in danger in the caliphate."

Curious and confused, I decided to call it a day and distract myself with a beer.

"Overthinking" I said to myself as I opened the fridge.

Chapter 7

As steady and silent as secret agents, we crammed our paperwork and personal possessions into convenient spaces and took up our positions in our vehicles. Subdued by the early hour and gravitas of the event, we left it to the birds hidden in the trees to express elation on our behalf for the beautiful summer dawning. Intense words and prayers had been exchanged at the church, tears suppressed by cheers, as relatives, friends, supporters, the Imam, the minister and his wife waited to wave us off after I had taken a group photograph; the first entry in my journal of our mission. As we moved off, vehicle by vehicle roaring into life as we began our advance, the emotion I felt was hard to figure out. It felt more like going to war than going for peace; it felt like being a part of something bigger than us; it felt like awe.

Even though we would see each other daily and often during the several days to come, Freya and I had already said a kind of goodbye of our own. In the past few days we had been more intimate, more demonstrative, more loving. I guess it was because we knew, even though neither of us put it into words, that for more than a week in our relationship we would be as chaste as friends and as detached as colleagues. Staring at the back of the ambulance she was in, I wondered what thoughts were going through her head, as we moved slowly out of the gates of the police car park and onto the road. Perhaps she was too busy chatting with Jamal and Saffi. Atif and I were sandwiched between her vehicle and Mo's, who as the Team Mechanic was assigned to travelling at the rear in case he was needed.

Atif and I were as mute as monks for the best part of two hours. I guessed that, like me, he must not be much of a morning person or perhaps, also like me, he was a little overcome by the intensity of thoughts and emotions as our journey began. He perked up after sipping some of the coffee I had brought in a thermos flask. Even though it had suffered in taste, I had ground the beans myself earlier and it was better quality than the instant stuff.

"Put something on that you like for a change, Dylan. Have you got a playlist on your phone? We don't need to be listening to my choices all the time. Anyway, it would be good to play something more lively."

We had been listening to an Islamic radio station almost as far as Birmingham; soothing, hypnotic melodies on a low volume setting.

I scrolled through my playlist, wanting something to recharge my mood.

"How about Queen's Greatest Hits?"

I felt an immediate, simultaneous jolt in my mind and chest; an internal, physiological slap of recognition of having said the wrong thing. I looked at Atif and was relieved to see he was smiling.

"Why not? Go for it," he said.

I did, but not before a private, mental acknowledgement that somehow my perspective had been tainted by a brutal ideology. As soon as I had named the band, visions of its brilliant lead singer being thrown off the top of a high building had flashed in my mind. It was an insight into what Muslims meant when they said that ISIS had hijacked their religion. But it was not enough to destroy my belief that love will always trump hate in the end, and my gloomy thoughts dissipated when we sang in full voice along to the lyrics. We were the Champions, my friend. We were having a good time, good time, good time, and wanted to ride our bicycles with gusto and glee.

The plan was to drive non-stop until we were south of London and free of the city outskirts before we stopped for lunch. After that it would be my turn to drive until we reached Dover. We hoped to rest for a few hours before our departure time of 5.30 p.m. to allow for any possible delays with the paperwork procedures and police searches, which had caused others before us to miss their scheduled sailings. Predictably, parts of the journey were smooth and went at a satisfactory speed; around the cities it became more sluggish and stressful. Still, we were happy with our progress and our timely arrival at the ferry ports as planned.

Thanks to the good work of Minister Tim and the Imam, a large group had gathered to greet us with gifts and good wishes. Some of the people were from what they described as a sister group of our InterFaith project, similar in purpose. Others had come independently from a couple of nearby mosques and churches. The rest had found out about us from Talkbook pages or word-of-mouth, and decided to come along to show support. It was humbling as well as touching to see fifty or more goodhearted people of different classes, races and faiths gathered there for our benefit. It softened the tedium of waiting for our papers to be cleared and our vehicles to be searched.

The questions the police at the port asked did not surprise me. We had all been briefed on the nature of the interrogations we could expect to encounter, and the officers were professional and polite in their manner.

"I'm sure you understand it is our duty to advise you against entering Syria," we all heard, as pamphlets were pressed into our hands by policemen with resigned smiles.

Bolstered by our well-wishers and looking forward to crossing the Channel, at first it took no effort to have patience. Then it required increasing effort until, just as we were about to lose it, we were cleared and finally allowed to get on the ship. Once parked in the claustrophobic, fume-clogged bays of the 'Spirit of Britain' it was good to stretch our legs, explore the ship's amusements and facilities, and breathe sea air out in the open.

Many of the travellers stood on the deck to watch as we left our home shores. The sun was still shining on the cliffs, deceiving us, causing them to appear as pure white as sugar, with a texture as soft as cotton. As they melted away in mist people wandered away, and Freya and I decided to find our way to the bow on an upper deck.

"Quick, while no one is looking," she said, clambering up on to one lower rung of the rail and holding her arms out. "Let's do a Titanic."

Laughing, I climbed behind her and threaded my fingers through hers, mirroring her posture; mimicking the famous scene in the film.

"Jack, I'm flying," she said in her authentic Irish accent.

Before we got to the kissing part she nudged me to get down, because the smell of burning tobacco alerted us to a smoker in close proximity.

Freya fished a huge bag of tortilla chips from her bag which we munched on our way to the bar. We took our sneaky beers to the window to watch the waves. We were still scraping out the contents at the bottom of the bag when Freya nudged me.

"Look," she said, pointing through the porthole with a finger crusted with yellow crumbs.

In the distance we could see the high-rise buildings of Calais looming beyond the beaches. We sucked the last bubbles of froth from our bottles and went outside to witness our approach to the French port. Large painted letters warned the monster we were sailing on to:

'KEEP WELL TO THE WEST.'

As we joined the throngs of passengers returning to their vehicles we spotted various members of our crew, merging with the drivers clattering down the steps to the parking bays.

Before we strapped ourselves into our ambulances Atif checked the map and confirmed the plan. "So now we take the main motorway to Belgium. We'll be stopping at the service station outside Bruges to eat and rest for the night."

"Roger. I'm just re-setting this for the hour we've lost," I said, fiddling with my watch.

It was a slow exodus from the ship as we rolled out on to French soil through the barriers and roads of the ports, picking up speed as we found the main highways. With Atif at the wheel again, I dozed between checking the landscape for anything of interest. It was mostly banal, but from time to time glimpses of a novel, historic culture stirred me from the hypnosis of traffic moving like animations all around me.

The setting sun was reflecting on the huge panes of the glass facade of the service station when we arrived there two hours later; transforming the ugly, ubiquitous architecture into something of beauty. Most of us wanted to eat before we prepared to attempt sleep. There was some pooling of provisions as we gathered with our leftovers; sharing sandwiches, samosas, potato crisps, poppadoms and some fruit, as we boiled water on our little gas rings to make tea.

"Bruges is supposed to be so pretty," Freya said, tucking her arm into mine, as we made our way to the main building with our towels over our arms, clutching our toilet bags. "We should make a list of all the places we pass that we would like to return to, on a proper sightseeing trip."

Near the shower rooms we bumped into Saif, and had our first friendly conversation with him about the outrageous prices of the snacks that were sold there.

The food, and the shower I took, hasty so as not to aggravate the HGV drivers waiting outside the booths, revived me a little, enough for the task of making my bed as comfortable as I could. We were all hoping for several hours sleep before we were ready to move on at sunrise. We shook out sleeping bags, brushed away stray debris from our supplies such as chickpeas and syringes, and laid out thin foam mattresses in narrow spaces, across front seats and cleared strips on the floor of the ambulances. Freya and Saffi had to squeeze their bodies into one such space.

"Good job we're petite," Saffi said, as they discussed the best arrangement with good humour and some experimentation.

As the sun climbed out from low clouds, filtering light over the prayer mats laid on the ground, Freya and I took our mugs of coffee a little way from the others to gaze at the sky.

"Hold this for a minute, " I said, handing Freya my mug. "I'm going to have to stretch out a bit. Aren't you stiff?"

"Not really. You should take up yoga with me."

When the ritual was over, Jamal walked over to join us.

"I'm making Asian eggs for our breakfast if you and Atif want some."

We were glad to accept because our alternative was porridge, and it was my turn to make it, for the first time in my life without a microwave.

By half-six in the morning, waved off in at least three different languages by admiring and encouraging holidaymakers, campers and lorry drivers, we were on the move.

"We should be outside Luxembourg before ten, Inshallah, so I think it would be a good idea if you took over the wheel for the first stretch, then I'll carry on until we have a stop off after Strasbourg. You can do another couple of hours after that, and I'll take over until we get through the Mont Blanc tunnel."

"Sounds good to me, though to be honest I'm a bit nervous because I've never driven on the wrong side of the road before."

"That's why I'm suggesting you get the hang of it on this part of the journey because it's pretty easy. Boring but easy, trust me. This road goes on forever, bro."

Atif told the truth, but the monotony gave me the opportunity to get orientated with the right-handed driving wheel and the left lanes. After three hours of clutching the wheel and concentrating too hard, I had developed a headache, stiff shoulders and more confidence. By the time we cleared the city limits of Luxembourg, my appreciation for half an hour's respite at a small café was disproportionate to the service. There was just time to use the toilet and down a milky coffee with a dry croissant, before I was back in the ambulance, happy to be in the passenger seat again.

The convoy eased back into France for the next leg of our journey. A few hours later we were cruising alongside the German border, several miles before Strasbourg, when Atif startled me out of my motorway stupor with a loud, long groan.

"No, no, no. This must be faulty." He jabbed his finger at the flashing fuel light on the console. "I can't understand it. Mo checked that we were all okay for fuel before we set off."

"So what are we going to do? Do you think we'll manage to get to our next stop?"

"I don't think so, that's nearly twenty miles away. Oh, man, we're going to have to pull over. Call Mo and let him know I'm going to stop in a few minutes."

As we came to a halt on the hard shoulder, our hazard lights flashing, a huge, intimidating truck beat Mo to it. Decorated in the colours and curling stripes of the Union Jack flag, it was cleverly painted to give the impression of fabric furling in the wind. Grunting and squeaking, it came to a stop behind us. A small, stocky man with a face like a pink satsuma, a shaved head, sleeves and a collar of tattoos jutting out of his vest, jumped out of his cabin with a friendly shout and an acrobatic thrust of his hips.

"Got a problem?" he said as we walked up to meet him.

Atif looked embarrassed as he explained. "Yeah, don't think the fuel gauge is working properly. We seem to be low on fuel."

The lorry driver laughed and shook his head. "Old

ambulance, mate? We'll see what we can do. What are you up to then?" he said, smiling at Mo and Abdullah who had joined us.

We introduced ourselves and told him about our mission. He put his hands on his hips and blew out a soft whistle.

"Wow, that's really something. I've got to hand it to you." Pete the truck driver shook our hands. "Now then, what I can do for you is siphon out some diesel which will get you as far as the big service station the other side of Strasbourg." He scratched his head. "The only problem is I haven't got the right equipment so I'm going to have to make do with a rubber tube."

Mo said he had one and ran back to his ambulance to fetch it, while Pete guided Atif in reversing ours as close to his truck as he could get without colliding.

"Christ, it's a while since I've done this," Pete said, twisting off his fuel cap and placing the rubber tube inside the hole.

We crossed our arms and cringed in silence as he placed his lips around the other end of the tube and sucked. He stopped, smacked his lips, spat on the floor, swore and spat out again.

"Bad?" said Mo, grimacing.

"Well, I wouldn't drink a pint of it."

Pete attempted to get the suction going again, but we were laughing so much he succumbed to the craic with a coughing fit and had to spit out again. On the third try the juice was flowing between the two vehicles and we all sighed with relief.

"This should keep you going until you get to the services. Maybe I'll see you there," Pete said, shaking our hands in turn, smearing a throat-catching souvenir of the smell of petrol on them.

"Mate, can't thank you enough," Mo said. "What do we owe you?"

"No, you're sound. Glad to give you a hand. With

something like you lot are doing that's good enough for me."

Pete was right; we passed by Strasbourg, filled up with diesel at the Services, and were overjoyed to see his patriotic lorry parked up there. We found him in the café, about to attack a triple cheese hamburger bloodied with tomato ketchup. He appeared to be torn between lust for his meal and pleasure at seeing us again. Abdullah, who had recognised a fellow Liverpudlian by his accent and was delighted on more than one account to see him again, asked if there was anything we could get him before establishing that he was a fellow Liverpool fan.

"Pete mate, have you been following the news about Mo Salah? I'm a bit out of touch since they signed him up last week. He officially starts first of July, tomorrow, right?"

Pete put down his oozing bun, his eyes firing up at the mention of the gifted Egyptian striker.

"Brilliant buy, brilliant buy, eh? What a coup, getting him. Can't wait to see what he's capable of."

We were all reluctant to say goodbye to Pete, not least Abdullah who had found a fellow spirit, but we had another seven hours or more on the road before we could call it a day. I was pleased that he agreed to a group photograph with all of us. Abdullah gave him his restaurant business card with the offer of a free meal, and we left Pete to his tepid, half-eaten burger and stiffened potato fries.

"Are you okay to drive until we get over the border in Switzerland?" Atif said, when we got to our ambulance. "We'll change places somewhere after Basel before the roads get too challenging."

Behind the wheel again, it was good to find myself enjoying the experience, which I put down to my increasing sense of competence, the less hectic highways and the breath-taking beauty of our surroundings. A few more scenic hours passed before we encountered another obstacle on our way. My spirits soared, resonating with the majesty of the mountains, particularly the highest, Mont Blanc. But the grating sounds from our weary retiree vehicles as they struggled with the ascent threatened to bring us down. They made it, and I thought the sensation of coasting downwards in that setting more exhilarating than any funfair I'd experienced.

"Okay, get ready for the longest tunnel you've ever been in in your life," Atif said, when he had paid the toll at Chamonix.

Being warned in advance could not prepare me for the seven mile stretch underground. The daylight at the end of the tunnel as we emerged into Italy was a comforting sight to me. It had been fourteen hours since we departed from Bruges that morning. Two hours later in a long and generous lay-by about twenty miles from Turin, we ate and prepared to sleep. Too tired for conversation, I slipped into quiet contemplation of the dimming gold and rose illumination of quilts of clouds, tucked into the valleys of the Alps and settling over the peaks, as the sun eased down behind them.

The symphony of light unfolding over the mountains at daybreak energised me more than coffee. Keen to get moving, we made breakfast quick and light. I was looking forward to fine Italian coffee and other local goodies during our planned break, about halfway en route to the port of Ancona. The further east we drove, past the gloomy carbuncles of the industrial areas, the prettier the landscape became. As we turned south the morning grew warmer and sunnier, and after four hours of driving I was primed for a pleasant interlude in the delightful seaside town we arrived at. We bought our fragrant coffee and paper bags full of pastries from the bakery, an appetiser for our next stop at a beach not too far away from the ferry port.

It was after three in the afternoon when we reached Seniglia. The temperature at that time was perfect, the golden sands dazzling, the Adriatic Sea pearly and promising. Of all the filming I had done, the scenes I shot there were the most fun, as I captured the childish holiday mood which had overtaken us all. We ate crisp and succulent pizzas which had been baked in ovens before our eyes, breathing in the aroma of bubbled cheese and fresh herbs. Then we flung off our sandals on the sands, and our cares in the waves. We had three hours to kill.

"This beach is to die for," I said, lying down and spreading my body, moving my arms like wings to leave an imprint of an angel on the sand.

At six o'clock, when the bell of a nearby church rang out, Freya suggested it was time to stock up on food and drink for the long boat trip ahead.

"I read on an online forum about the ferry that there is only a little snack shop on board and that was closed, so we don't want to take any chances do we? Besides, it will be nice to take fresh bread and cheese and fruit. I'm going to get another big pizza."

We all agreed and traipsed up the decking path to the showers, shaking and brushing off sand from our skin and hair.

The glorious respite of the afternoon had made us optimistic, which made the confusion and chaos at the ferry port of Ancona a greater disappointment. We attempted to make sense of the random hand signals of the men in yellow vests and white helmets, until we found the right lane and waited to board. The ferry ship looked like a floating white fort as its two drawbridges were lowered. For two hours we crawled along, stopping and starting, with motorhomes, camper vans, and cars dragging caravans, observing giant lorries making complicated manoeuvres in order to reverse into position in the HGV bays, assisted by the frantic arm waving of port operatives.

Atif turned the engine off once we were parked in our assigned tight space.

"This don't look like no cruise, bro," he said, which

gave us some comic relief.

Upstairs, as we looked around at figures and rucksacks sprawled over the available seating, and travellers huddled under 'No Smoking' signs puffing on cigarettes, we began to wonder if the extra expense of booking cabins for the eighteen hour journey might have been worthwhile.

"We can always sleep in the ambulance," I said, knowing by the look on at Atif's face that he did not fancy the prospect of sleeping in the bays below any more than I did.

When we set sail at nine, Atif and I decided to wander around for an hour until the sun set.

"Let's find the girls first then explore the ship," I said.

The 'girls' found us first, just as we were about to take the stairs to the upper deck. When we reached the top, Atif got excited.

"Things are looking up. Luxury," he said, running up to the swimming pool taking up most of the area.

Close up we discovered it was waterless.

"Like a mirage," Atif said.

I was more disappointed than I would have expected.

"Aw, man, that would've made a big difference."

What was satisfying to us was to find an area of seating that was almost free of other passengers. We claimed as much space as we could with our bags and jackets.

"You stay here and guard everything while I go and tell the others," I said to Atif.

When all of our crew were either assembled at, or had been informed of the site of our occupation, we took turns to go back to our vehicles to fetch sleeping bags and pillows, toilet bags and towels. The benches were hard but preferable to a night in the airless bowels of the boat, and we were compensated by the kind weather conditions. An empty row of seats formed a barrier between Freya, Saffi and Jamal and the rest of us. Before the light was gone, I took photographs and a short recording of our camp preparing for the long, dark night on board. Freya mocked me when I reached the back row, lying on her sleeping bag and stretching her arms over her head with a contented yawn.

"Special privileges, eh?" I laughed at her pulling her tongue out. "A whole row to yourselves. Sweet dreams, Princess."

She blew a kiss to the camera.

I woke several times before I decided my hours of sleep were over. I sat up and rubbed my face, eager for the sun to show up and show me what the night had hidden. The emerging beauty of the shining coastline and islands, embraced by the flashing sea, exceeded my expectation. Ahead of us a large body of land rose from the water like the back of a giant whale. I guessed it was Corfu, and the eager prospect of passing between that lovely island and the mainland reconciled me to a further five hours of sailing, before we reached Greek soil at Igoumenitsa.

Chapter 8

Not even the captivating splendour of our surroundings could compensate for the sense of captivity. Our food rations dwindled and our impatience grew as the morning dragged on. Finally, we approached the docks at Igoumenitsa without any announcement from the control room. I gathered up my bundle with relief and joined the stream of passengers stampeding down the stairs to their vehicles.

"Oh no, it's Sunday, remember?" Atif said, when we were seated in our ambulance, waiting to move off.

"All day. What's the problem?"

"The shops and stores, as well as the supermarkets will be closed. Hopefully, we'll find a kiosk or minimarket to buy enough to keep us going."

Edgy with hunger and frustration, we gave up on conversation as we endured another hour of laboured progress before we were out of the port and onto the main A2 route.

"That's better," I said to Atif, when we had finished our snack of milk, biscuits and fruit from a little roadside shop. "I'll drive if you want."

"No problem. The plan is to make a detour after Ioannina, about an hour's drive. We'll leave the main road and stop at the nearest village to find somewhere to get a proper meal."

If the mood that characterized our Italian experience had been light-hearted and frivolous, in Greece I can best describe it as a feeling of full-heartedness; a joyful filling-up of gratitude for the generosity and kindness we encountered. It began soon after we rolled onto and through the old, cobbled streets of the Zagori village. The old houses we passed had irregular slate roofs, and were made of light-grey stone that looked white from a distance in the radiance of the afternoon sun. The moment we pulled up on a stretch of rough ground next to a beautiful, ramshackle, ancient church, its bell sang out four peals. Atif got out to find someone who could approve our parking there, before we left our vehicles in search of food.

Through one of the arches that ran alongside the length of the church, a tall man with a long, grizzled, frazzled beard appeared, wearing a long, black coat-dress and a gold cross that tapped his stomach as he walked. He stepped out and waved, smiling and calling a greeting to Atif. The priest reached out for my friend's hands as they met, and listened intently to what he was trying to convey. Knowing Atif spoke no Greek, I was relieved to see that Atif clearly understood the priest's reply. He held out his hands in a gesture of permission, and then walked off towards the village square.

"What a lovely man," Atif said, as he returned to where we had been watching his interaction under some olive trees. "He speaks pretty good English, and told me we can stay here as long as we want. He's just performed a Baptism ceremony for two babies. He says they're having a celebration in one of the kafenios. There will be plenty to eat and drink, and he's sure that, especially when the people hear of what we are doing, it would make them very happy and be an honour if we joined them. He said if we walk up that little street it'll be really easy to find them."

Atif went on to convince us that the priest was very sincere, and that the villagers might consider us churlish and ungrateful if we refused to accept the invitation as graciously as it was given. We followed him like disciples, smitten already by this enchanting place nestling below pine-decked mountains, and the heart-warming reception we had been given.

The kafenio was brimming with adults and children of all sizes and ages, platters of food and pitchers of drink, and bursting with laughter, chatter and lively Greek music. Any shyness we had was soon dissolved by the friendly manner in which we were welcomed and pulled into the festivity. Proud mothers, aunts and cousins in party dresses pointed out the babies. Grandmothers in plain black frocks offered us savoury pies that melted in our mouths, glasses of refreshing juice, and beer, which only Freya and I accepted.

I had lost all sense of time, until Saif annoyed me by reminding us we had been there for over an hour. He had not stayed at the party, but had gone off with Rafeed and a few others he had persuaded, to find another kafenio. Atif said that his excuse was that he wanted more choice of food. Returning, he popped his head through the door, called out a few names to attract attention, held up his arm and tapped his watch. Making our way out, we said our reluctant goodbyes, repeated thanks, wishes that we could stay longer, and promises that one day we would return. The villagers smiled, hugged us and patted our heads, and we knew that they understood. As we stepped out into the street, three old ladies in black headscarves each held out a few cake boxes to Freya and Saffi. They opened up the boxes on top of each of the three piles to give a peek of what was inside; more of the local pies, pastries dripping with honey and fresh bread rolls. Another woman scuttled up as we thanked them, holding out a jar of honey in one hand, in the other a pot of marmalade, which she placed in Jamal's hands. Freya was in tears, as she accepted the gifts and kissed the crinkled cheeks of the kind women.

Although we did not want to leave we knew we could not afford to be delayed. Our intention was to stop overnight near the town of Kavala, at least another four hour's drive from where we were. Six ambulances moved off before us. Atif and I waited to move out behind Jamal's, but after a few minutes of hearing the engine's feeble cough on starting, followed by a splutter, we knew something was wrong. We also appreciated the wisdom of having Mo at the back of the convoy, ready for such an emergency. Through the walkie-talkie system we had in place, he communicated to the others that we had a problem.

"Go ahead and wait at our rendezvous in Kavala, in the car park of the Lidl supermarket which would be closed. If it looks as if it's going to take longer than twenty minutes to fix the problem I'll let you know. There'll only be an hour at best to find a place to stay before dark, once we get there."

Mo lifted up the bonnet of the ambulance with Abdullah's help, and Atif went back to the village in search of assistance. Knowing I could not be of any help, I followed Freya and the other two to the bench in the little olive grove near the church. Freya raised her eyebrows when I pulled out a packet of Greek cigarettes and a lighter from my pocket.

"Where did you get them from?"

"From the little kiosk near the port. Don't worry, it's just for the trip. I thought they'd take the edge off my hunger, and they were so cheap it'd be rude not to. Those are my excuses anyway."

"What are you like?"

"Want one?" I offered Freya the pack.

"Uh-oh. Don't tempt me."

I walked away from the women to a spot behind the stone church wall to savour my guilty smoke. When I rejoined them, Mo was scratching his head, talking to Father Dimitri, or Papa Dimi as we had learnt to call him at the party. The priest appeared to translate Mo's words to an old man standing by his side. He had a cheerful face, the colour and texture of nutmeg, and white straggly, monkish hair. He was wearing crumpled baggy clothes and tough boots, in front of which lay a big canvas work bag. Abdullah came over to us and explained the identity of the priest's companion.

"That's Papa Dimi's handyman and church gardener. He's also the chief car mechanic of the village."

It was fascinating and quite entertaining to observe Mo

and the old man set to work on repairing the vehicle, communicating in the language of their practical expertise, which required no Greek or English.

From our bench we cheered when we heard the healthy growl and hum of the engine returning to life. After our saviours had cleaned their hands with baby wipes, the thanks, prayers and promises were repeated with even greater feeling, and our three ambulances set off towards Kavala. We made good time, and when we turned into the supermarket car park where the other seven were waiting Naz told us they had only been there for twenty minutes.

"There's more good news. When we got here a German couple in a campervan had stopped for a break and to find their bearings. They spoke perfect English and told us they were booked into a campsite by the beach at Nea Karvali. It's only a few miles away. They've stayed there before, and found the owners very kind and helpful. The toilets and showers were not the best they said, and told us it was best to bring our own food, but there's a kitchen to cook in. Cheap and cheerful was how they described it. Anyway, they called the site to check there was space for us to camp overnight. There is, and they gave us the site's number and their own, and instructions on how to get there."

Our convoy set off to Nea Karvali at once.

The blue of the sky was beginning to marble, running into streaks of pinks and reds, deepening the terracotta of the roofs of white apartments. We passed between palm trees lining the roads, admiring mountains to our left and glimpses of sparkling sea between buildings and trees to our right. In less than ten minutes we drove between the wooden gateposts of the site, where a man was waiting to offer us a friendly welcome. We presumed he was the owner, tipped off by the German couple who had explained our needs. Naz, near the front, got out to talk to him. I guessed the campsite owner knew some English as he prodded at the piece of paper in his hand because Naz was nodding as he spoke. We learnt via the walkie-talkie that the owner was happy for us to stay overnight.

"Gets better, guys. He's only going to charge us ten euros per vehicle. That's less than half the normal fees for that time of the season."

In return we were prepared to squeeze our ten vehicles on the square of brown, struggling grass he directed us to, where on average there would probably be no more than six. As he guided our ambulances into position with exaggerated hand gestures, a middle-aged woman who looked like his twin sister waddled up to his side, flapping her apron. When we had gathered round them for introductions, we learnt that the pear-shaped lady with the same long, olive face and thick, cropped, black hair as his was his wife Zoe, and he was Theo.

It only took a few minutes for our hosts to show us round the sparse facilities of the site, then Freya and I decided to walk the short distance to the shore. We were just in time to catch the last embers of light turning the sea to liquid gold before the day's end.

"How do you fancy getting up an hour early in the morning for a swim and to watch the sunrise," Freya said.

"Why are you whispering? I'm up for that. Up at five then? Let's go before the trail gets too dark to see our way, although it'd be good practice for tomorrow morning."

We kissed good night out of sight of the campers. As we approached the shower block several of our group were straggling out. Naz, toweling his hair, called out to us.

"Hey, if you need a cold shower you've come to the right place."

On our patch, others were brewing tea and sharing out the honey cakes gifted to us by the generous Greek village women. It was enough to keep me going after the huge afternoon feast. I was ready to sleep and even the brisk shower I took made no difference.

It was my turn to sleep on the front seats of our ambulance. When Freya tapped on the windscreen just after five in the morning, I was ready, in swim shorts and sweatshirt with my towel around my neck, to flip-flop back to the beach. We held hands, taking our time on the path, cautious because the light was poor, and many loose stones and sharp things slowed us, pricking the soft soles of our feet. On the narrow strip of sand and pebbles we huddled close together, smoking my Greek cigarettes. Spellbound, we watched the glow spreading from the Eastern sky overlay turquoise onto the lapis lazuli of the sea.

Freya jumped up, kicked off her flip-flops and tugged off her sweatshirt.

"I'm going in."

I did the same, but hesitated, rubbing my bare arms and chest as she plunged into the waves, shouting out at the shock.

"Ah, come on, you big wuss," she said, cupping her hands to splash me with chilling cascades of sea water.

I edged in, gasping, before hurling myself into the currents.

"Jesus, you could've warned me. It's friggin' freezing."

Awakened and exhilarated, we swam and played until the sun and our time was fully up. Our frolic had been child-like and our embraces seemed shy when we held each other close for a few minutes, before we dried and dressed our shivering bodies.

"We'd better go," I said, reluctant to pull away from the heat of her skin. "The others will be getting ready to go soon."

In less than a week we had grown accustomed to the conditions of participating in this mission.

Atif had prepared breakfast of coffee and the bread, marmalade and honey we had been given. As we were tidying and packing up in order to leave, the Germans, Noah and Leah, approached Abdullah who was by his ambulance, next to ours. They were carrying a big basket of eggs and five loaves.

I heard Leah say, "We have been to the bakery in the village and got these for you."

Abdullah took the gifts from them, offering payment which they refused.

"That is so kind. I'll make omelettes for lunch if some of these peeps will give me a hand."

"We wish we could come with you," Noah said.

Abdullah put his arms around the German's shoulders.

"One day, Inshallah, one day."

We climbed into our ambulances and moved off, smiling and waving to the thoughtful couple.

"Auf wiedersehen, danke," I called out of my window, echoed by Freya from hers.

The driving schedule for our fifth day was ambitious; twelve hours or more on the road, into and through Turkey before we stopped for the night somewhere north of the city of Aksaray. It took us through varied landscapes.

"Get ready to say goodbye to the sea for now, Atif said, not long after we had emerged from a lush National Park.

Near the town of Iasmos, we stopped to buy fruit from a cheerful, toothless old man who was selling his produce in wooden crates by the roadside stall. Atif got out the map and pointed to our location while we munched his mouth-watering apples.

"So, only about thirty miles from the Bulgarian border as the crow flies East?"

"Right, and we're doing well. Not long before we'll be in Turkey."

Before midday we had crossed the Turkish border and left the main road to park by the northern shores of Lake Bahsayis. On the outskirts of Istanbul, it was surrounded by opportunistic industrial and residential developments crowding its slopes, creating an incongruous contrast to its waterside beauty.

Abdullah was as good as his word, and with the help of several volunteer assistant chefs, dished up a delicious meal.

"Guys, that was so good," I said, wiping my bowl with a crust of bread. "I just wish we had more time to relish it."

Saif, who had taken on the role of our unelected timekeeper, spoke up. "That's right. We need to set off by one o'clock if we want to get to our overnight stop on time, rather than winging it."

Nobody told him he was right but we all got up to help clean up after the meal.

The dense architecture crawling all over Istanbul was dignified in my eyes by the magnificence of the ancient churches and mosques, standing tall even when dwarfed by modern high-rise towers. Gleaming boats on the glorious Bosphorus Strait sailed beneath as we swept over on the bridge above. Listening to the midday calls for prayer washing over the city, we parted from it. Away from the metropolis, some of the scenery was not dissimilar to Greece, I thought. The further we travelled into central Turkey the more rural the landscape became. The ethos grew more conservative, apparent in the dress and demeanour of the people we passed on the roadside or working in the fields. During our brief stop for a break and to swap drivers, I heard the call to the afternoon prayers echoing from a distant, unseen mosque.

A few hours later, when I had taken over the wheel, Atif held a conversation over the walkie-talkie.

"Get ready to turn off the road towards Tuz Gölü, Dylan."

I followed his directions to the great salt lake; the stunning location we were looking forward to making our venue for the night.

"Oh my God. Would you look at that?" I said, at my first sighting of the vast white plains of glittering salt crystals. I pointed towards the handful of people stepping gingerly through the snow-like shallows.

"It makes you expect to see skiers and snowboarders."

We found a space large enough for us all to park and jumped out, exclaiming at the spectacular scene. At the edge we removed our sandals to dip our tentative toes into the strange, saline soup. I picked up a formation of salts, the size and shape of a snowball, and thought of lobbing it at Freya. She saw me and laughed, lifting up a warning finger.

"Don't even think about it."

Close-up, the water sparkled the palest pink, a hyper-diluted hue of the flamingos I could see in the distance, like faraway flames. I felt as if I was walking on water.

With salt stinging and clogging up the spaces between our toes, and crusting the skin on our feet up to our ankles, we went back to our ambulances to clean up as best we could without wasting too much water. After much brushing we resorted to baby wipes and a final rinse off with our precious rations. The consensus was that we would prepare our evening meal where we were so we could watch the sunset. Then we would find a better, more sheltered place to stay; prepared to sacrifice toilet facilities and even meagre comforts for a night by the lake.

Before our banquet of pitta bread stuffed with hummus, fresh salad and fruits, I sat, mesmerised, in my camping chair. The sky and lake were transformed into two bands of rich colour, which made the blood oranges and grapes set aside for our dessert seem like crystallised droplets from them. The full moon appeared with slow grace as the lights faded, closing the show with a silver screen. I was ready to sleep and looking forward to the spectacle of the sunrise. It pleased me when we only had to drive a few hundred metres to find an ideal space between two hills, and I wasted no time settling into my makeshift bed.

The sun rose with the same flourishes of vivid corals and blues as it had closed the day before, garnishing our meagre breakfast of leftovers. Feeling blessed by the experience made me no less keen to find somewhere with toilets, a place to sit down for coffee and something more substantial. Most of the drivers were in their ambulances when I felt the need to relieve myself.

"Hang on a sec, Atif. I'm going to have to take a leak."

I jogged around the small hill to dissolve some salt. Making my way back around the curve of the base of the hill, I saw someone squatting, smoking and speaking into a mobile phone. It was Rafeed, and although I could hear his words I didn't understand them. I was sure the language was neither Arabic nor Urdu, which Atif and several of our crew spoke. I was thinking it was probably Bengali, when I heard a word I understood clearly.

"Kalashnikov," Rafeed said, before speaking in the same language as before.

I was as shocked as if someone had pointed an actual weapon at my face

"Night vision goggles" were the next distinct words I heard from his lips, before his smoke wafted to my nostrils, and caused me to cough. As he swung round to look at me, I prolonged and exaggerated the cough to distract him. I laughed and clutched my throat with one hand, flapping my other in the air, hoping he would laugh too. He did, but his eyes were louring.

"Are you okay, bro?" Atif said, as he drove us away. "You seem a bit quiet."

The words I had overheard played over in my mind. I decided not to share them. They could mean anything; something; nothing. They were none of my business, I told myself.

"No. I mean yes, I'm okay. I'm just looking forward to a loo and sitting down at a table to eat."

In the café we found further on by the lakeside, I was reassured by Rafeed's good humour. He seemed as relaxed and refreshed as the rest of us, sharing bread and chatting as we finished off our Turkish breakfasts of goat's cheese, boiled eggs, olives and tomatoes.

"Will you come with me to buy some of those melons

before we go?" Freya said to me.

I went outside with her to the stall next to the café. The farmer cut two generous slices from a melon and invited us to sample them.

"Oh, my goodness," Freya said, as she swallowed her first mouthful of the luscious smile.

I sunk my teeth into the fruit, sucking up the juice. It was wonderfully sweet, an unexpected taste in a world of salt.

The third discrepancy between my expectations and experience that day occurred several hours later, at the Reyhanli refugee camp in the Hatay province of Turkey, not far from the Syrian border. I had heard reports of Turkey turning a blind eye to, and even facilitating, the passage of jihadists and arms through its borders. What had I had not appreciated was the extent of the hospitality with which its government, with the help of the United Nations and NGO's, had catered for the needs of the refugees. I had expected to see tents, but not the neat, well organised rows laid before me with the large green initials of the Turkish Charity printed on the white canvas. I had anticipated crowds of displaced, traumatised people; fear, misery, injury and impoverishment. There was all of that if I looked for it for sure, but I also felt the force of compassion and resilience as I walked through the camp. I was surprised to see classrooms, nurseries, laundry rooms and play areas.

There was an aura of innocent joy around the smiling children who approached me, curious and playful around my camera. A little girl held my hand and swung it. Others performed dances, and boys demonstrated clever football skills, for me to capture for eternity. They brought a sense of normality, defying the horror of the circumstances that had brought them there. Later, when I lay on my camp bed that night in the tent provided for us, the thought of those irrepressible young souls gave me hope.

Chapter 9

With the dreamlike, haunting chants of the pre-dawn call to prayer the background melody to my half waking, half unconscious thoughts, I searched for the smiles of those children through the gallery of other faces playing through my mind. A man blinded by shrapnel, a young woman with staring, unseeing eyes who had her sight but had lost her mind in slavery, a twelve-year-old girl waiting for a prosthetic to replace the leg taken by a bomb, a mother in a wheelchair nursing her baby, burned and scarred faces and bodies. Who knew what scars thickened in their hearts, minds and souls?

I recalled voices from the previous evening; offers of tea and food as we walked towards the dining room, words of welcome, introduction and enquiry, sometimes in English from educated Syrians, and the stories told to us by volunteers. Eating the rich, spicy stew, freshly baked rolls and side dishes of vegetables, rice, beans, and grape jelly so delicious we could not imagine how something so good could be made out of so little on little gas rings or fire pits. We had taken our dinner with several of the camp workers from different countries and with different backgrounds; some students, two retired teachers, a doctor, a dentist, a psychologist. The doctor and the dentist explained that a lot of the treatment needed was for chronic, existing conditions as well as for those caused by the violence of war. For all, we were told, medical equipment and supplies were insufficient to cope well. Freya and I were chatting with the Canadian psychologist, Susan, when I expressed my amazement and admiration for her and her colleagues, and the resilience of the refugees.

"It's their spirit that keeps me going and makes me feel humble," Susan said. "What matters to me most is the children; their lost lives, their education. Contrary to what you might hear on the News, most of these people are escaping fighting on both sides. The only side we are on is Peace."

"But how do you cope with all this tragedy?" Freya said.

Susan shook her head.

"Sometimes better than others. I've had to learn to take care of myself if I'm going to be any use to anyone else. I guess I've trained myself to look for anything good, even the smallest thing, and focus my attention on that. But that can take a lot of work, believe me." She paused for a few moments, chewing her food with her eyes closed, then looked at us and put her bowl down. "An example, my worst one," she said, "was a teenage boy who had been drugged and kidnapped by armed militants, not the army, who removed his kidney. They harvested his kidney to sell on the black market."

We had no words, and were comforted when Susan began to recount more uplifting stories to which the other workers contributed.

The faces and the voices mingled in my consciousness, alternately amplifying and receding, fading and drifting away as sleep reclaimed me. Not for long, it seemed, as the second call to prayer stirred me and the other four bodies in my tent to life; signaling time to prepare for the new day that lay ahead. I washed as best I could with the cold water, the domino-sized bar of soap and a rough square of flannel. Walking towards the aroma of coffee and fresh bread coming from the open Staff Kitchen, I reflected on the different roles assigned to the members of our convoy for the last day of our mission. Even though I was looking forward to my work of interviewing, photographing and videoing the residents of the camp, especially the little ones, I could not rid of myself of a chronic pinch of envy. It arose from my desire to be going into Syria; to where the situation, and therefore the plight of the people, was most urgent and dramatic. It was hard for me to relate to the attitude of several members of our crew, who were adamant they had no wish to go that far.

My first task of the day was to get some footage of the ambulances, our drivers and those who had arrived to escort them into Syria before they departed. I was surprised to find the prospect of saying goodbye to our vehicles quite a poignant one. Freya agreed, when she came back to my tent after breakfast to help me carry my camera and equipment. The tent was empty so I got a kick out of the bonus of a stolen morning kiss. I presumed Atif and the other two I had spent the night with had already gone to their ambulances. I was right, but when we reached the group of our drivers and Jamal, who were standing talking to ten male strangers, I noticed that Naz had moved apart from them. He was crouching on the dusty ground clutching his stomach, his features squeezed with pain.

"Naz." Jamal had spotted him too when she saw us running towards him. "Are you okay?" She required no answer as Naz raised himself to a low squat, twisting to one side to divert the explosion of vomit from his mouth away from us. "Right," she said, helping me as I put my arms under his to lift him up. "Let's get you back to bed and get the doctor to look at you. There's no way you can go into Syria this morning."

Naz shook his head and groaned, accepting the baby wipes Freya was holding out to him to clean his face and the spatters on his shirt and jeans. Then he began to retch again, and allowed Atif and me to lead him back to the medical centre; luckily for us without throwing up again on the way.

"I'm going to have to find someone to take his place now," Atif said, after we had left Naz with a doctor.

"Me."

Atif ignored me as he began first calling out names, then looking inside each of the four tents we had been allocated. They were empty; all the beds stripped, no personal belongings to be seen. "Where are they all?" he said.

Our enquiries brought us most of the answers but not all. We found the three who had spent the night in Naz's tent also in the medical centre, being treated for vomiting and diarrhoea. Two others had already set off early for home, taking a taxi to the bus station in Reyhanli. No one knew where Saif was.

"That just leaves me then?" I couldn't help but grin, even though the circumstances were unfortunate.

Atif looked down, lifting and dropping his shoulders, and sighed.

"Looks like it. But I think it's best if you leave your camera equipment behind."

It was already thirty minutes later than the intended departure time when we got back to the ambulances. Looking back, I wonder if the solution of substituting me for Naz would have been so readily accepted if frustration and impatience had not infiltrated the waiting team.

"So you got what you wanted," was all Freya said when I told her the news.

I asked her to take my equipment, which she basically knew how to use, and do what she could with Saffi to take my place for the day. I could see she was holding back tears as well as any comments about my decision, when I held her close and whispered in her ear.

Atif read her thoughts. "Don't worry, we'll look after him. All being well, we'll be back this afternoon. I'm guessing we should be back by four at the latest."

Jamal agreed, reminding Freya that we were only making a hundred and twenty kilometre round-trip into Idlib province. "Not so far. Allowing for the stop-offs for deliveries, I'm sure Atif is right."

Her brother gestured for our escorts to join us. "Okay, so let's get the introductions and the photos out of the way so we can get going."

"Assalamu alaikum," we all repeated, as names and handshakes were exchanged with the six Syrians from the

Sham Civil Guard and four others, of Dutch, French, Belgian and British nationality, referred to variously as humanitarian workers and activists. The drivers were assigned to us on the basis of how much Arabic we could speak. For me that was zero, so Shaki, the aid worker from East London, was to be my companion.

When I took my camera out to set it up for Freya, a salvo of cigarettes hit the dust. The Sham Civil Guard guys smoothed down their vests with the logo of their brand on the backs, collected their white helmets from the back of the pickup truck they had arrived in, and put them on for the group photograph. That done, the pace quickened. We were urged with shouts and gestures to take up our places in our ambulances, leaving me just seconds to squeeze Freya's hand and say, "See you soon. Love you."

"Yes. Stay safe. Love you too."

"Is that your girlfriend?" Shaki said, as I clambered in next to him and we moved off, waving to her and Saffi, standing with the little group of adults and children from the camp who had come to see us off.

"She is, and she's the one who really got me involved in this."

"Is that so? How come?"

Shaki seemed interested in the InterFaith project and the story so far as I told it.

"So this is your first time in Sham as we call Syria? Did they tell you that this is probably the last time you'll be able to do a convoy like this?"

"Not for definite, although I've heard it said that charities are having to find new ways to deliver aid, and I guess ambulances."

"Exactly right. Crackdowns, mate. They're all cracking down. We don't even know if we'll get through the Turkey border without any problems these days. It used to be a breeze but not anymore."

"Why is that?"

Shaki shrugged, lifting a hand from the wheel. "Politics.

Terrorist threats. Pressure from the Allies. Who knows? It's all up in the air. Some days it's easy, some days it's a hassle."

It was a relief to discover that this was an easy day at the Bab al-Hawa crossing, where the Turkish soldiers, with bored expressions and dismissive gestures, allowed us through after a cursory check of our passports and loads. Shaki's shoulders relaxed and he lit another cigarette once we were clear of the border gates.

"Right, I'll just run through our route with you, and hopefully give you an idea of what to expect."

He listed the towns and villages where our six drop-off venues were located, and explained about the checkpoints operated by the militants in the area. Then his conversation became more general, even friendly. He seemed to like to talk, describing his parents who had emigrated from Pakistan in the 1960's, his upbringing in East London, and his three brothers and two sisters who were still there, with good jobs and families of their own. He had had a variety of jobs.

"Nothing special, he said. "I was even a rapper at one point. But see, what really changed things, when I turned thirty about five years ago, was getting into this volunteer aid business. At first I just did it for several weeks or a couple of months between jobs, gigs or whatever; Afghanistan, Iraq, Libya and now here. Two years ago it had grown into a full-time job, so I set up my centre and brought my wife and little son over. He was only two at the time."

"So how have they adapted to it?"

"Not too bad, not too bad, but I'd be lying if I didn't say my wife and me weren't looking forward to going back home one day. How about you?"

"Well, I just finished uni a few weeks ago so I guess I'll be looking for a job when I get back."

"Cool. What did you study?"

My instinctive hesitation before answering worried me.

"Multimedia Journalism."

Shaki took a drag of his cigarette and threw back his head to exhale.

"A journalist, eh?"

Atif's caution about my camera equipment came back to me.

"Not really. Not yet anyway. I haven't really decided what I want to do." I decided to lie in that instance. "I've got a packing job working in a warehouse at the moment."

"Been there, mate. Okay, well, we'll be coming up to the first checkpoint before Sarmada in a few minutes."

I looked ahead at the same, plain road we had been travelling on, passed only by a few cars, some vans, the odd lorry and several motorbikes on the other side. In front of me was the back of the ambulance Atif and Jamal were in. Around me, beyond the verges of rough terracotta soil was a barren landscape dotted with shrubs here and there, behind which loomed hills like shadows. Occasionally we passed a few grey, intact but nondescript oblong buildings, displaying no sign of residential or commercial life.

We were slowing down. Shaki must have sensed my apprehension as we approached the checkpoint. "Don't worry, I know most of these guys."

When we came to a stop I could see to the left of us a ramshackle portakabin, where four men with rifles slung over their shoulders had begun asking for and perusing passports. Rafeed was the only one of us who had got out. He was laughing and chatting with one of the militants, holding and stroking the man's AK-47.

"Rafeed's Arabic is really good," I said.

Rafeed looked up towards me, then said something to the armed man, cocking his head in my direction. They both stared at me for a few seconds, then the militant spoke to Rafeed again, who nodded in reply.

"Okay, we're good to go."

Shaki handed me back my papers with a reassuring

grin, and turned to speak some friendly words in Arabic to the man who had checked them, slapping him on the shoulder and saluting before he turned on the ignition. The tension that had been building in me, as I watched papers being passed to and from each ambulance, drained away, leaving me with a weak sensation in my muscles. As expected, four of the vehicles took a left hand turn further down the road, and a few hundred metres on, another three turned right. Depending on the nature of our supplies, we were heading to different places. When deliveries were completed, we were all to meet again at a rendezvous point about five kilometres from the border, where two members of the Sham Civil Guard would return us to the refugee camp in two of the ambulances.

Passing through the towns and villages near the border, I had been surprised at the bustling ordinariness of life there. No damaged buildings to be seen, just people getting on with life; old men playing card games outside tea houses, women in headscarves and long dresses shopping, sometimes with husbands and lively children. As we got closer to Sarmada I saw more evidence of the ravages of war. Broken buildings, barely standing, with rubble spewing out of their guts, and glimpses of streets with carpets, quilts and bedsheets hung on clothes lines crossing them. I imagined noisy houses of families hoping for, caring for, neglecting, taking for granted and appreciating the homely comforts of those soft furnishings.

"I'm going to speed up a bit here," Shaki said, as we entered the town. He pointed up at the rooftops. "Snipers. Got to be careful."

There was little traffic; the odd lorry, a few dented, dusty cars and more regularly, passing motorcycles carrying men, some with pillion passengers in burkas. I observed that I had seen a lot of motorbikes and many males, but few women and children since I entered the country, and was hopeful to see more of both when we reached the centre which Shaki had told me was our first stop.

I was to be disappointed. The yard where we pulled up and unloaded some of our supplies into a storage shed was empty, apart from an obese man in a dishevelled tunic and baggy trousers who shuffled over to us, scratching his debris-flecked beard. He addressed Shaki first, nodded to me, surveyed the stack of supplies we had delivered, and showed his approval by raising one hand and his eyes up to heaven, muttering in Arabic. Then he threw his short arms around Shaki's, shook my hand and wobbled back through the main entrance of the building. Shaki explained in general terms that it was now an aid headquarters. I could see it had once been a school, but it had no glass in its windows and certainly no children. It had lost its soul. Its playground had been made hazardous with craters, its walls scarred by shelling. In a corner, where I pictured children playing the Syrian equivalent of hopscotch and other games in happier times, was a contraption I thought I recognised from social media images as a 'hell cannon.'

Shaki got back in the ambulance and told me to join him.

"Everyone is busy today, but the clinic staff based here will be very grateful for our delivery," he said.

I asked him where the children were. He shrugged and looked at his watch. "Maybe some of the boys are at religious school, or at the gym. Anyway brother, we've got to keep to time."

Our next destination was a small hospital on the outskirts of Al Dana. The two ambulances carrying Mo, Atif and Jamal with their two drivers had waited in the street for us, and began moving slowly as we turned out of the yard. We had only been driving for five minutes when we were forced to a crawling pace, then to a halt as a roadblock appeared ahead. It was created by two plastic barriers, the kind I had seen at home, erected by Highways Maintenance men for roadworks. This one was manned by four gunmen dressed in camouflage trousers and flak jackets, with cloth wound around their heads, nose and mouth, concealing most of their faces but not their hostile eyes.

"This is new," Shaki said, in a tight voice which betrayed his nonchalant words.

The gunmen waggled their weapons, indicating that they wanted us to get out of our vehicles.

It all happened quickly. I understood nothing, only that those armed men demanded to see our passports and papers, speaking to Shaki in aggressive tones. He seemed to be remonstrating with them as they handed back everyone's paperwork except mine, and ordered the others with fierce gestures and shouts to get back in their ambulances. I will never forget the faces of my friends at that moment; ashen with shock and panic, their eyes and mouths wide open in silent screams. The two White Hats drivers were calm and obedient. They ushered their passengers back to their seats, and with deliberate haste got behind their wheels, turned on the engines and fled. At the sound of a vicious snarl from the leader of the gunmen, Shaki muttered an apology to me without looking at me and did the same. Then my hands were tied at the same time my sight was taken away.

Chapter 10

A hefty shove between my shoulder blades propelled me forwards and I stumbled. Stooping, I managed to get to my feet, then my chest was compressed between two hard, burly arms lifting me and flinging me onto a hard, scratchy surface of gritty, splintered wood. My nose landed first, and I wondered if the slime oozing from my nostrils was blood or snot.

"Move," a voice said in what sounded like a Russian accent. Chechen more likely, I thought to myself as if it made any difference. I crawled forward until the crown of my head hit something which clanged. A thud, a grunt and the shaking of the floor underneath me was followed by more metallic slamming and rattling. I guessed I had been thrown into the back of the pickup truck I had noticed at the checkpoint, with my brutal Chechen guard for company.

Reason tried to assert itself over the fog spreading through my brain. They have made a terrible mistake, they will realise and everything will be resolved soon, it said, but my thoughts were scattered like shrapnel, and I could only hear the quiet, clear whisper of my instinct telling me I was in deep trouble. With no opportunity to channel my fear through fight or flight, I succumbed to the urge for survival by drawing up my knees and curling my shoulders into a fetal position to protect myself against any blows that might come my way, or at best the discomfort of travelling at high speed over rough, bumpy roads.

It was not a short journey, although if I could guess I would say it took less than an hour to arrive at our destination. I focused on my breathing, attempting to slow and deepen it, to bring it down from the rapid, shallow rhythm beating high in my chest. When the truck rumbled off the tarmac to what felt like softer terrain, I heard several voices call the Islamic greeting in different accents, and my breath quickened again like a racer's. Big hands gripped my arms like iron vices, contorting my shoulders into a painful twist as I was pulled off the back of the truck with my legs flailing to find solid ground. Through the sound of my pulse pumping in my ears I heard someone say with a Birmingham accent, "Well, what have we here?"

"A spy," said my Chechen guard.

Another Birmingham voice spoke. "A spy, is it? You don't say?"

Other speakers join the conversation which was then conducted in Arabic. Judging from the differences in cadence and pronunciation, it seemed to me that as well as my two countrymen they came from different countries, and were not natives of Syria.

It made sense to me, however grim, that one of the Midlands pair should be tasked with taking over the care of me, for want of a better word.

"Watch your step, mind," my new keeper said in a sardonic voice as he led me forward by my arm, cackling as I tripped over a drop in the level of the ground.

The dimming of the light behind my blindfold, the change in the quality of the air and the temperature as we stepped down, suggested to me that we were going underground. Moments later my impression was confirmed when my blindfold was ripped off. I was confronted by the confines of the tunnel we were in and the big, round face of my captor, whose large rodent-like grin was framed and encroached upon by matted, black hairs poking out of the mouth-hole of the balaclava he was wearing. We were standing before a heavy, black painted metal door with an oblong grid of metal bars at eye level; several inches wide and perhaps a foot high. It seemed to me like something I'd seen in cartoons; a precursor of many absurd thoughts to follow during the course of my confinement.

"Make yourself comfortable," my minder said in a droning mumble heavy with sarcasm.

He chuckled as I looked around the tiny, empty

concrete cell, realising that when the door was closed on me I would be alone in gloom. The only light I could hope for were the feeble rays of the lighting in the tunnel reaching me through the bars in the door. Where would I get air? In a corner of the room, under the low ceiling, I could just make out a square opening cut into the wall, covered with mesh, before I was pushed inside and could see nothing. The full weight of the door slammed behind me. I listened to the sound of its locking and the shuffling footsteps moving away without a word.

Feeling my way to a corner of the room, I slumped to the floor, hugging my knees and resting my forehead on them as if they would help me bear the heaviness of my thoughts. When speculation about the reasons I had been brought there, the purpose of the militants, the conditions and treatment I might face, and the prospect of my future became too terrible to endure, I felt myself surrender to a numbness creeping over me. I don't know how long I remained in that state, until the stiffness in my limbs and a painful pressure in my groin forced me to stir and get up. Again I used my hands to guide me round the walls, until I was standing in front of and peering through the spaces between the bars in the door.

"Hello, hello," I shouted as loud as I could muster, in the manner I might use to get the attention of an absent shopkeeper. It sounded ridiculous and inappropriate, and brought no response.

"Brother," I called. I put my ear to the grid, repeating my plea. "Brother." I listened again and thought I could hear a door opening somewhere further down the tunnel. It was quiet for a moment, but when I cried out "Brother" for the third time I was shocked by the sudden, quick stamping of footsteps towards me. I stepped back in fear as a key was rattled in the lock and the door was flung open with a violent push. The next brutal swing of the arm that opened it was aimed at my face. I felt and heard the impact on my jaw along with the words, "I am not your brother."

My meek, querulous apology added to my humiliation.

"I'm really sorry, but I don't know what to call you and I'm desperate for a pee. I didn't think you'd want me to do it in here."

"For a start you don't have to call me anything. But any road up, you can just call me Doctor because that's what I am. And for all I care you can wallow in your own piss."

His words surprised and depressed me, so that when he adjusted the AK-47 on his left shoulder and grabbed mine with his right hand to lead me through the door I felt gratitude. Before I was allowed to pass, squinting, through the entrance, the Doctor called out in Arabic a sentence that sounded like a warning. Several figures of different heights and girths, all armed with automatic rifles and all with their faces covered by balaclavas or scarves, except for their eyes, stood still in the courtyard of a complex that looked as if it had been hewn out of the rock, watching me. The Doctor pointed at a cracked wooden door in the smallest of three concrete buildings with his weapon.

"Thank you," I said as he pushed me through the door with a hefty thump and shut it behind me. The toilet was clean; a small but significant comfort. It consisted of a ceramic squatting pan set in the middle of the concrete floor, with a small length of hose pipe attached to a tap on an adjacent wall to sluice it and wash. My relief when I used it was so strong it felt for a few seconds akin to brief waves of pleasure in a sea of despair.

I took the precaution of knocking on the door when I was ready to leave rather than making a normal exit. The Doctor opened it, and again using his weapon to point my direction, we made our way back. We passed some vehicles parked in the courtyard; a small digger, a pickup truck I imagined might be the one that had brought me there, an ambulance with the 'White Hats' logo on its side and another with Arabic lettering on the back window. I wondered where our ambulances were; whether everyone had or would get back safely. With sadness I thought of Atif, and with unbearable sorrow about Freya when he delivered his news of me to her.

The Doctor's Birmingham comrade followed us back to the cell. There were two doors near the opening of the tunnel; the one on the left was open, and when the Doctor noticed me looking inside he pushed my face forward with the back of his hand. All I had chance to see was a saline drip with the NHS logo on the plastic pouch of liquid, next to one of two hospital field beds, and a shelf with trays of bottles, boxes and dressings.

Back in the cell, the Doctor told me to sit down in the centre of the room. I sat cross-legged like a yogi, while they paced in circles around me, swaying their Kalashnikovs in a bizarre ritual. In other circumstances, in a different context, I thought the pair might make a good comic double act. One tall, thin and lanky, who spoke in slow, lugubrious tones, and the Doctor with his protruding belly, short, lean legs which did not match it, and his quick, grandiose manner of speech.

"So you're a spy?" the Doctor said.

"No. Never. I came only to deliver aid to help the people. A humanitarian mission."

"So you say. Why did you bring all that camera equipment?" the other said.

"We thought it would be a good idea if I kept a photo and video journal of our trip to show what it's all about, maybe publicise the situation, raise awareness, do some good. That kind of thing."

The Doctor shook his head and scraped his front teeth with his index finger nail.

"But we've also been told that you said you were a journalist."

"A student. I studied Multimedia Journalism but I haven't got a job. I mean, I don't work as one. Just in a warehouse as a packer."

The medic's sidekick batted the back of my skull hard

with the back of his rifle.

"Admit it, you're here to report back to your Western masters."

"Not true. I came to help." What could I say? "Surely you can understand that? You must have come here for your own good reasons?"

"You can say that again," my abuser said. "It wasn't possible for me to stand by and do nothing while my brothers and sisters are being mown down like cattle."

The Doctor joined his fingers, pointing them upwards, muttering something in Arabic.

"Yes, I had to leave behind my work in the National Health Service, my job in a hospital and my life in Birmingham to fulfil my holy duty too. For ten months I lived without my wife and baby son."

"That's hard." I meant it, but I was feeling my way to establishing some kind of relationship with my captors if I could; some point of empathy. "Are they here with you now?"

"Alhamdulillah, they are."

Encouraged, I continued. "Are you both doctors?"

They both found the question very funny.

Pointing at his friend, his big belly heaving, the self-professed Doctor said, "Him, you could say he's a Pharmacist. He used to deal in drugs."

The friend stopped laughing with a murderous stare at the Doctor, who changed the subject.

"So you're from Northern Ireland, eh? Well, you should know something about freedom fighters, then? Whose side would you be on?"

Cautioned by the throbbing in my jaw, I paused before replying; wondering whether it was a trick question, whether there was a right or wrong answer.

"You mean the Troubles? To be honest, most of what I know and understand about all that has come from my Grandad, who actually experienced it. And he's not one to take sides. He says there was evil done on both accounts, and the only way to achieve lasting peace is to acknowledge that."

Wrong answer and too much of it, I guessed, as I fell forward on the concrete with the offence-driven force of the second blow to my skull.

"Ignorant kuffar," the Doctor said, lowering his weapon. I was left alone to recover.

I shuffled myself back until I was leaning against a wall, and began feeling the back of my head; relieved that despite the pain there was no blood. I needed strategies to survive, I decided, and seeking the smallest snippets I could feel grateful for was somewhere to start. Beginning with the absence of blood, I rejected worries about swelling and concussion. I turned my attention to the consolations that my body was intact and it looked as if I wouldn't be forced to go to the toilet in my cell. I was working on being thankful for being left alone without threat or harassment for the time being when the Pharmacist returned, shattering that train of thought. At least he's bringing a little light into the situation, I thought with some irony.

"I need to get some information and email addresses from you so we can get in touch with your friends and family."

His words were at the same time poignant and frightening to me.

"What do you mean? What for?"

"We need to let them know where you are and why we are holding you. We need information that only you and they would know to confirm your identity."

"Why are you holding me?"

"Apart from you being a spy, maybe somebody will be willing to pay up for you."

I wondered how much I was worth, not that it mattered, because I believed that whatever amount was demanded for me, it would be hard to raise it. The Pharmacist asked me questions about my childhood and my loved ones; each one an infliction of torment. When the prodding was over and my interrogator had a list of nicknames, places and pets, he asked me for the hardest things to surrender; the email addresses of my mother, sister and my girlfriend. It was darker when he left.

The next time I heard the stomping of boots down the tunnel and the clanking of the door, I braced myself for worse to come. I recognised the gruff bark of the Chechen as he entered, and thrust a piece of flatbread half-wrapped in foil and a plastic bottle of water into my hands.

"Thank you," I said, as he locked the door and tested it with a shake on the other side.

The bread was dry and plain but I savoured it, and the water was so welcome it could have come from a mountain spring. I wanted to drink it all but the uncertainty of knowing when I would get more stopped me, as well as wondering when I would be allowed to go to the toilet again. I had no idea of the real names, backgrounds or histories of my kidnappers so I gave them identities of my own, whether accurate or not.

My next visitor came with light footsteps, opening the lock with quick, deft fingers. The jihadi used his phone as a torch, allowing me to see his beautiful, unnerving eyes, neither kind nor cruel, through the gap in the fabric wrapped around his head and face. North-east Asian, I thought, and mentally named him the Uyghur, drawing on some of my research about the conflict. Whoever he was, he was appreciated for the foam camping mat and two blankets he flung into a corner of my cell.

"Thanks, I'm really grateful for that. Is there any chance I could go to the toilet?"

His response was blank, so I said "bathroom," pulled a face to show urinary discomfort, pointing my finger at my groin and the door. He nodded, took his rifle off his shoulder and used it to guide and hurry me with rhythmic pokes through the twilight, to the toilet and back. There was no sign of his companions which made the operation a little more relaxed than the first. Warplanes grumbled in the distance, accompanied by explosions and the rapid retort of gunfire. Thank God they are not close, I thought.

As the Uyghur turned the key I sank to the floor, crawling my way to my bedding, wondering how I could keep my mind away from the most awful imaginings, and if and how I would be able to sleep. I decided I needed tactics and some kind of routine. I told myself this might be a good time to master meditation practice, and considered what kind of exercise I might do. Physically I felt weary but mentally I was jittery. Taking deep, long breaths in, holding and releasing slowly to calm me, I devised a series of stretches which I intended to repeat in the morning after waking; something to get started. The stretching made me feel better so I lay down on the foam mat and made a cocoon of the two blankets around me, with a rolled up corner under my head. With my eyes closed, I began to play the Abundance Alphabet game, as I had done a few times before when I had trouble getting to sleep. It involved working through each letter of the alphabet, first thinking of good things I already had in my life, evoking them, and then visualising other things I desired to have or do in the future. For A, the image that came into my head was Atif, smiling and joking. If I focused on his smile it helped to keep away the hurt, so I did the same with D for my sister Dolores, and Em. I conjured up vivid mental movies of holidays to Africa, Bali, the Caribbean and Cambodia. For D, Damascus came to mind first, but I settled on Denmark, and to be back in England for E. By F, I was falling; after Freya and freedom.

Chapter 11

There were two loud, high-pitched screams which felt as if they vibrated through every cell in my body, followed by a silence during which I tried to work out if the sounds were in my head or outside it. Clarity came after a few moments, when a series of more intense shrieks followed, coming from somewhere close, beyond myself. Creeping up to the metal grid in the door, following the wall with my palms, I squinted in the mean light into the tunnel. Ahead of me, two silhouettes were manhandling a large, lumpy bundle through a doorway. As I watched, the lump groaned and grew limbs as it was lifted and bumped between the walls. From the shapes of the men moving towards me, I guessed they might be two of the unidentified Arabs I had heard when I first arrived there. I stepped away from the door, in time to avoid a collision with it as it was flung open with the projected weight of the bundle, which landed at my feet. One of the carriers kicked it out of the way so they could close the door.

Through the light-coloured T-shirt on the hunched back of the man who had been deposited before me I could see wet streaks; creeping stains that, although it was too dark to see colour, I knew were red. Not wanting to touch him in case it caused him more pain, not knowing how I could help him or what to say, I stayed still and stared at my tragic cellmate for many minutes. When he lifted his head up a few inches and raised a hand in the direction of my bed, I crouched next to him. As gently as I could, avoiding his wounds, I eased him across that small space. Before he rolled in slow and painful increments onto his side upon the mat, I noticed stripes of dark liquid oozing on the bare soles of his feet.

When the Chechen entered the cell a short while later, the only acknowledgement that I had a companion was the two flatbreads and bottles of water in his hands. When I had eaten my bread, I wrapped up the other piece adding my half of foil, and sipped some water before standing up to go through my stretching routine. Tears welled up and burst in my eyes as I raised my arms above my head for the first move, hearing my Dad's voice saying, "Just keep showing up, son. Just keep showing up."

I was squatting next to the body, holding the water bottle close to his lips as a prompt to drink, when the Uyghur surprised me by appearing at the door. His hooded eyes seemed half closed in the half-light as he bent down to place two apples at the side of the door frame. He backed out through it, sealing us in and departing with the same discretion as he had arrived. As I hopped over to collect them, I wondered if the apples were a happy accident because he and the Chechen had not liaised, or a gesture of compassion.

Happier still when I turned round, was the sight of the brutalised man sitting up on my mat, concentrating on the tentative extension of his arms and legs one by one, as if he was testing their function. I asked him if he was alright, and to my pleasure and surprise he answered in clear English that he was.

"You speak English?"

"I do, and maybe when I'm in more in the mood for a friendly conversation, I'll tell you why."

I handed him the water bottle, liking him already for the fact that, despite the wicked treatment he had endured, his dry reply suggested he had retained a sense of humour.

When he had drunk a little water, he examined his feet and asked me to lift off his T-shirt to check the weals on his back. Although it was a good sign that they had stopped bleeding, they were sticking to the cotton of his top, which made it a slower, more excruciating process for both of us. I peeled the fabric away from his flesh, pausing and biting my lips when he flinched.

"What do you think? Not so deep, not so bad?" he said.

I confirmed that there seemed to be no deep gashes, mostly areas where the surface skin had been ripped off.

"What did they do to you?"

"Cables. Whipping. Torture just for the sake of their jihad, I suppose, because they know I am no longer a fighter and I have nothing new to tell them. Do you know my screams are music to the ears of the Mujahideen, my friend?""

"You used to fight them?"

"Not them specifically. Daesh. ISIS. I am a Kurd. I used to be a soldier in the People's Protection Units, the YPG."

"Yes I've heard about that. So what you do now, where do you live?"

"My name is Xarabat. From 2011 to 2013 I fought with the YPG until I was injured and I had a chance to escape to England. My cousin is a barber in Mancaster city centre, and he fixed it so I could go to live and work with him. I wanted to come back last year to fight in the battle of Kobani but he stopped me. He had friends who were killed trying to cross over the border by Turkish soldiers."

"No way. That's unbelievable. I'm from Northern Ireland but I've been living in Mancaster for the past few years too. If I'd have known I could have got a haircut from you. So that's why your English is so good. But why have you come back now?"

"I came back a month ago to see my mother. She lives in Afrin near to her two married sisters and close to one of mine. I had to come to see how she was because she has been sick. She is getting older and I was worried about the Turkish Army activity in the Canton. She was okay. She said she was safe and refuses to leave her village, but I think someone tipped off the Turks about me. For some reason, after they arrested me they decided to hand me over to these goons. Maybe my best hope is that they'll use me for a prisoner swap."

"Aren't the Americans supporting your guys, the Syrian

Democratic Forces?"

"For now, yes. As long as we are useful I think. It's complicated, as they say. Maybe they don't want to upset Turkey too much? Who knows? You know we Kurds have a saying: we have no friends but the mountains."

What struck me most about Xarabat was his grit. It was stamped on his broad forehead, his high cheekbones and his square jaw; framed in his broad shoulders and compact, muscular build. His strong face was handsome despite the veins of blood shot through the whites of his brown-green agate eyes, which sparked with the fire of defiance as he spoke, and the dark crescents of strain underneath them. Looking at the black stubble that darkened his skin around his mouth and chin, I rubbed my hand over the scratchy beginnings of my own beard. His haircut was fashionable, not unlike my own, with a thick thatch of hair on the crown; sleek and razor-cut close around the ears and the back of the head.

"We could both use a trim," I said. "Maybe when we get back to Mancaster."

If they decided to hand out the same treatment to me as they had to Xarabat, I wondered if I could cope as well as him. To turn my thoughts to something less disturbing, I found the two apples. Polishing them on the inside of my polo shirt which looked cleaner than the outside, I smelt the odour of my own sweat in my armpits. Handing an apple to Xarabat, I asked him if he could manage to eat something yet. "If you can, there's some bread here for you." I felt for the foil package and placed it next to him.

"Hey, and you're in for a treat. I actually think I tasted cheese in this one. They must have forgotten the olives."

It made me feel good to know I could make him laugh.

Breakfast came to an abrupt end as I was nibbling on the apple core, picking out the last bits of flesh with my teeth. Up to that moment, the sounds of warplanes we had heard often had always been muffled; distant and unthreatening. At first nothing seemed different, until the noise of the jets amplified, piercing through the armour of our cave.

"Russians? Syrians?" I said.

Xarabat was looking up, listening.

"Could even be the Americans, taking an odd pot shot at some Al Qaeda pals they've fallen out with."

He put his finger to his lips and listened again.

"It's over us, man. Hunker down."

Pulling up his own foam mat, he pushed me to make me release mine. He crossed his legs then made a roof of his mat. Hunching, with both hands crossed over his head the way the airline safety cards show you, he urged me to do the same.

There were three drops, landing with earth-shaking impact a second before each of the bombs exploded, shattering matter, rattling our bones, almost bursting our eardrums. I cowered under my mat, praying as I felt the weight of each piece of fallout that nothing heavier would come down on my head and crush me. When the attack ended, quiet and fragments of dismantling structures descended around us. The alarm over, the only sound I could hear was the ringing in my ears until Xarabat's voice came through. I opened my eyes and saw the light.

"Dylan. Dylan, are you okay?"

"I think so. Are you?"

"Yes, Alhamdulillah. Look at the door, look at the door."

It had been blown away by the powerful forces from the sky.

"Thank God," I said. "Thank God."

"Don't get too excited. We're alive but we're not free yet."

"I meant thank God because we could easily have been under that."

Able to see my way, I clambered over the mounds of rubble and pieces of concrete that had erupted from the walls of the tunnel into our cell. We had to shift a large amount of debris with our hands before we could make our way further; determined that we could do it because of the sunbeams making their way from the outside world to us.

Worried about Xarabat's injured feet, I made him wear my sandals. I put on the thick wool socks that I had found beneath my blankets, making me suspect the Chechen had a soft streak too.

"I insist. It'll make it easier for you to move and you don't want to get an infection. Besides, my girlfriend says I must never, never, ever wear socks with sandals."

I adjusted the straps for his smaller feet.

"True. Not cool. Thank you, my friend."

Xarabat smiled at me and patted his hand over his heart before we pushed on.

Of the two rooms I knew about in the underground structure, one had completely imploded and the other, the clinic, was half destroyed by the collapsed roof, under which one hospital field bed and half of another were crumpled and broken. Amongst the dust and fragments lay NHS saline pouches popped like balloons, ribbons of bandages, a layer of glitter made from scattered glass and coloured pills sprinkled over the scene like vermicelli.

Together we heaved away a loose beam crossing the entrance and, exchanging congratulatory smiles, stepped out into the courtyard. Our elation was soon deflated by the thunder of boots running towards us, and shouts of "Yalla, yalla." The first to reach us was the Pharmacist, who pushed us both against the wall and pressed the butt of his AK-47 into Xarabat's right temple, followed by another athletic jihadi who did the same to me. In seconds we were surrounded by four more masked figures, including the panting Doctor.

As we were swung around and shoved in the direction of the concrete buildings, I noticed that there were now two ambulances in the yard, into which two stretchers were being lifted, accompanied by the manic calls, gestures and movements of several men in White Hats surrounding them, making it impossible to see the features of the wounded. With their covered faces, it was difficult to identify individuals, although the ones who attended to us most often had become familiar. I glanced around at the group escorting us, and apart from the Brummie brothers there were four I did not recognise. The Chechen and the Uyghur were missing, and I realised I wanted them to be saved.

Our new premises of confinement were in the building next to the one that held the toilet. As the Doctor fumbled with a heavy chain and padlock to open the door, which was scored with shrapnel but intact, I noted with a wisp of relief that the toilet had survived, although its wooden door had lost a plank, was skewed and half off its hinges. Inside, the floor we were dumped on by our angry guards was still only plain concrete, but we saw that our prison had a few advantages over our previous one.

The Doctor commanded us to stand and, shouting through the door, summoned someone in English. A short, emaciated male in a balaclava stepped forward, answering in a French accent with a squeaky voice that convinced me he was still a teenager. As he carried out the Doctor's instructions, I noticed that the little black scarecrow was trembling as he chained my left hand to Xarabat's right wrist, my left foot to his right ankle. Muttering under his breath, the Doctor tested the chains then slapped the youth's thin shoulder, indicating that they would leave us.

"Upgrade," Xarabat said, pointing with his free hand at a narrow, oblong window high on one side of the front wall where daylight was pouring in through the chicken wire that took the place of glass.

I could see that he was mentally measuring its dimensions as I was.

"Maybe it's time we went on a diet," he said.

We managed to coordinate our movements, using the

other to support our bodies to get on our feet and practice shuffling around the room.

"I was never any good at the three-legged race," I said, then had to explain.

Xarabat was amused by my description of my primary school Sports Days, and in turn gave me a humorous account of some of the games from his own childhood.

Continuing our commitment to do our best to look on the bright side, we discussed devising some exercises appropriate to our shackled state as we practised moving together with more ease. It kept us occupied and distracted from the noisy, busy activity outside. The trundling and scraping of the digger, the rumbling of vehicles coming and going, and the constant bellowing of the labouring Mujahideen. When we rested, I reflected on whether the quiet of the underground cell, which I had found oppressive, had been better than the intrusive din.

Eventually the environment grew calmer. As the sun had moved we guessed it was no longer possible to carry on in the heat of the day, and the workers had retired for lunch and perhaps a siesta. We were grateful when one of the Arabs came in with water for us. Xarabat asked him if we could use the toilet, to which his response was to unchain us and lead us at gunpoint outside. Our shadows were longer, meaning it was later in the afternoon than I had thought. The yard was empty of humans and vehicles, apart from the resting digger in the corner. I wondered if the ambulances had been back since the morning and if any of the patients had returned after treatment. The toilet door had been put back on its hinges. It was still wonky and had to be lifted into place, but at least it provided privacy. Inside, all the dust had been swept out and the cubicle hosed down. I used it first, and as I was waiting for Xarabat with the Arab, whose rifle was pressed between my shoulder blades, the Doctor and the Pharmacist appeared from around the block and marched towards us.

Xarabat came through the toilet door. The Pharmacist raised his own AK-47 and pointed it towards him, while the Doctor began talking to the Arab in loud and vehement tones. I did not understand, but I sensed dissent as the Arab shook his head and shrugged, pushing me in the back with his weapon as a sign to walk back to our jail. The Doctor flounced away, talking to himself. The Pharmacist came with us. He stood on guard as the Arab put the chains back on our hands and feet, and remained with us when the Arab left.

It soon became apparent when the Doctor appeared at the door that the calm after this morning's storm had not improved his mood. His vindictive fury induced by the air raid was blazing strong.

"You see how those infidel swines destroy our hospitals and even our schools," he said, throwing up his arm and pointing his index finger to the sky.

His rant did not worry me most. I was too scared by the pair of knives he was holding in his other hand. The Pharmacist said nothing as he stood over us with his arms folded and his legs spread apart.

The Doctor's prophetic rage became more hysterical as he spoke.

"You have sown the seeds of your own destruction."

Taking slow, deliberate steps he began to walk in circles around us, stopping to sharpen his meat-chopping knives with long, nerve-crunching strokes close to the back of our bent necks, so that the sound of metal grating rang in my ears and made every hair on my body rise and stiffen.

"So, are you ready to meet your God?" he said, stepping in front of us and using the tip of each blade to lift our chins to meet his boiling eyes. He laughed and addressed the Pharmacist. "Hey, isn't this how our brother said they did it in Bosnia?" He simulated sawing his leg just above his knees with the serrated edge of his knife. "Or maybe," he said, straightening up, "we will just barbecue your skin."

My heart felt as if it was contracting in the centre of my chest; the blood in my veins running cold and sluggish. The sudden opening of the door made me start. My jumpiness amused the Pharmacist but the Doctor looked annoyed by the return of the Arab, who beckoned them to follow him outside.

Xarabat nudged me and whispered, "They don't want me to hear. They know I understand what they say when they speak in Arabic. And believe me, that is fine by me." He began taking deep breaths in through his lungs until his belly was extended, and waiting for a few seconds before releasing, so I copied him until I could feel my anxiety easing. "I hope the Doctor feels better now that he's got all that off his chest," Xarabat said after a few minutes, when I was relaxed enough to smile.

Later, when we were beginning to feel relief that the ordeal was over, and more confident that the gruesome charade would not be repeated again that day, the sound of someone manipulating the chain and padlock at the door caused rockets of tension to launch inside me. When I saw the face of the French teen, or the Belgian Kid as Xarabat called him, probably correctly, it was a welcome sight. He was carrying two bottles of water and a rattling cardboard box which he put down on the mat between us, before creeping off with his quick, angular movements and closing and securing the door.

"Mmm, potato fries," Xarabat said, pulling off the lid of the box and picking out one of the contents, pretending to blow on it as if it was hot then putting it in his mouth and chewing it. "Bit salty."

"Chips. You can't beat good old chips," I said, counting out our portions.

"Yeah, pass me the ketchup."

"I will if you tell me where you put the vinegar."

Our crunching was louder in our ears than the sounds of faraway fighting which started up again. Each time we heard a warplane Xarabat gave me an estimate in kilometres of its distance from our location. "You know, Xarabat, I'm beginning to believe everything you tell me."

He tapped his nose. "Very wise, my brother. As I am four years older than you, I am the wise old man." He cupped his ear and listened. "Now that could be as close as five. Maybe they are getting closer." We carried on listening, with him making guesses until the numbers grew larger and we felt safer. Xarabat told me that the Syrian Air Force did not have the capacity to carry out bombings at night, and so far the Russians had not been inclined to.

When the skies grew quiet, the Belgian Kid returned to allow us to visit the bathroom before night fell, as Xarabat had requested. Our shadows were long, Xarabat's was shaky and I noticed he was limping more. After we were manacled together again and seated alone on a mat, he eased off my sandals to inspect the crusty, sticky soles of his feet, which he told me he had just rinsed in the toilet.

"How are you feeling? Are they painful?"

"Not too bad. I'll be fine after I get some rest. You could say it's been a bit of an eventful day."

"Just a bit. But how are you going to get any sleep like this?" I shook our chains. "You can't lie on your back, can you? You must be sore."

Xarabat looked up at the window on the opposite wall where the rays of the dying light were straining through. "Come over with me to the door."

Supporting each other, we synchronised getting up, hobbling over to the door and kneeling up together in front of it as Xarabat instructed. Reaching out his hands, he ran them around the wooden panels, feeling the surface and from time to time picking at it with his fingernails until, with an exclamation of muted triumph, he held up a long thin nail.

"Keep still," he said, inserting it into a tiny gap in the padlock that held our hands, and wiggling it around.

In just a few minutes I felt the snap of the mechanism

release and the chain loosen. It took Xarabat less time to free our feet.

"Brilliant. Amazing, man." I felt excitement and fear. "But what if they catch us?"

"Well, we either take that chance or risk no sleep, which isn't going to help us hold it together, is it? We don't have to worry until the morning, and then we'll hear them coming. In the meantime, we'll be hidden under the blankets, and can fasten them up first thing."

Xarabat sounded confident which reassured me, and I appreciated the freedom of walking back to our mats and arranging our bedding without being yanked and contorted. When we were settled, me on my back and Xarabat curled up on his side with the chains between us, I explained the Abundance Alphabet method to him. "It's a game my girlfriend taught me to help me sleep. The letter X can be a bit tricky but I usually go off before I get to that."

"Not for me, brother. I will play it in Kurdish. And if I get to the end, I can think beautiful things about myself and many good X words we have."

He closed his eyes and I wondered how knowing this man for only one long day could feel like a lifetime.

In the sense that any sleep is good in such conditions, I slept better than I had expected. I hoped Xarabat had too when I lay fully woke, watching the faint glow of dawn grow over the door, wondering how many hours between fits of wakefulness I had been blessed with. The trundle of heavy wheels rolling into the yard outside made me sit up, fully alert. Xarabat's eyes opened wide, staring and listening with me to the slamming of metal doors, thumps on the ground and urgent voices. "Looks like they're making an early start," Xarabat said, flinging off his blanket and springing over to the door. "What the hell is going on?"

Although Xarabat's broad shoulders looked to me more capable of bearing the weight of a grown man, he insisted that he climb up on mine to spy on the activity outside. Leaning with my lower back against the door for extra support, I had just bent my knees for him to step up when the surface behind me became a wall of sound. The whoosh of powerful jets of water hitting it, like waves crashing around rocks in a storm, filled the room. As Xarabat lifted his face up to the gap it was sprayed through the mesh which made him wobble for a few seconds, hurting my shoulders. Then someone must have turned the pressure down because the cascade was less forceful and shouts of "Yalla, Yalla" could also be heard.

"Be careful." Xarabat, pressing his head against the side of the window, kept a cautious watch for what seemed like a long time to me before allowing me to let him down.

"Very good of them to provide a shower for us this morning," he said, wiping droplets off his face with his hands.

"What's going on?"

"Wait. Shsh, listen."

The shouts and splashing had ceased. We listened for a few minutes before Xarabat gestured for me to crouch down again and let him get back up.

"Just for a minute this time," he said as I hesitated before doing what he asked.

I counted sixty seconds before tapping his calf to tell him his time was up.

Xarabat jumped down and pounced back, landing on his sitting bones on his mat, which he patted for me to join him.

"I can tell you what I saw but I can't make any sense of it. But first, let's get attached again before anyone comes in now the show is over."

When my body was mirroring his, he draped and fastened the chains around our wrists and ankles as gently as if it was a rite of bonding, and we leaned back against the wall for the storytelling. He told me that there were two pickup trucks and an ambulance in the yard, with

111

about fifteen people, men and children who looked like ordinary civilians, sitting and lying on wooden pallets placed in the middle of the yard.

"No women?"

Xarabat shook his head. He said that there were four members of the White Hats; two of them operating the hoses, one behind the camera filming the whole operation, and another who seemed to be directing the proceedings. Children stripped of their clothes and topless men were being sprayed with water. Xarabat demonstrated how the Doctor, dressed in a green medical tunic, was yelling into the camera and pumping with manic vigour the back of an flabby male floundering under his hands. Xarabat said he heard shouts of "Gas" repeated several times.

"Then I got down. When it all went quiet and I looked out again, the water was turned off and everyone was dressed. The children were smiling because some of the jihadis were giving them handfuls of something from bowls, maybe treats. The Doctor's resuscitation must have worked because the fat man was sat up rubbing himself with a towel and laughing."

"Sounds mental. So what do you think all that was about?"

"Who knows? Maybe they forgot the bubbles."

We fell silent when we heard the familiar clunk of metal at the door. I couldn't help the lift of my eyebrows and the smile coming to my face when the Chechen walked in. But I wondered if I had been careless in letting him see I was pleased to know he had survived yesterday's bombing. His right arm was encased in plaster from his wrist to his armpit; from his left shoulder hung his Kalashnikov. In his left hand he held a plastic bag containing bread, which he threw on my lap before drawing out a bottle of water from each of the pockets of his camouflage pants. As he turned to leave, I whispered to Xarabat.

"Should we ask him about the Uyghur?"

With a frown and a slight shake of his head Xarabat

declined.

When the Chechen had gone he explained.

"It's not good to let them know we are thinking anything about, or taking an interest in their personal identities. As long as they keep their faces hidden from us, I think there's a chance we'll stay alive."

Breakfast was generous by the usual standards; it was a full loaf which we decided to eat half of and save the rest for later. We were chewing on our portions when the door was opened again, and the Chechen reappeared, holding a small bowl covered with a neat pile of fabric in his good hand. He placed them on the mat between us, speaking in Arabic to Xarabat and left us once more.

"They're giving us a change of clothes," Xarabat said, lifting them off the bowl. "Things are looking up." He showed me the contents of the bowl; figs, dates and pistachio nuts. "We even get the party leftovers."

A little overwhelmed by our good fortune, we were considering how much of our luxury foods to eat and how much to stash when we were surprised to hear the sound of another visit. This time the Belgian Kid entered, followed by a tall, hefty stranger whose frame almost filled the doorway. Because of Xarabat's earlier words, I was glad to see that his face was also covered apart from the eyes, and astonished at the startling blue irises staring at me from pale sockets. He greeted us in English, in an Australian accent.

"So, an Irish man and a Kurd."

"And an Australian walked into a bar," Xarabat said.

I winced at the joke, but the Australian ignored it. With his forefinger he prodded Xarabat's head, which was at the level of his own chest.

"America's bitch," he said with a sneer.

Xarabat, at last knowing when to shut up, nodded and lowered his eyes.

The Belgian Kid held out the orange bundle he was carrying.

"Put these on," the Aussie said.

Xarabat took them and pointed at the other clothes we had been given.

"What about these?"

"All of them. We'll be back in a short time." The Aussie ordered the Belgian Kid to unchain us.

When they had left, Xarabat spread out the white T-shirts and sweat pants, all made from thin fabric, and the orange boiler suits on our mats.

"Going for the layered look, it seems."

I could not speak; I had seen the orange uniforms in media images of ISIS beheadings although I could never bring myself to watch the snuff videos, and I knew their significance. We dressed in silence.

It was not the Australian who came to collect us as we had expected, but the Doctor and the Pharmacist carrying large, industrial spades which they handed to us and made us walk, each with an automatic weapon pressing on our sacrum. With each step, through the yard, out of the compound, up the slope of the hill out of which the underground bunker had been carved, to the brown, poor grassland at the top, I felt my strength draining away.

"This is your own grave you are about to dig," the Doctor said in a solemn voice which did not conceal the vibrato of his sadistic pleasure.

The violent pounding of my heart against my ribs felt like the ticking of a grenade about to explode.

"No whistling," Xarabat said, picking up his spade.

Can he not help himself? I thought, are wisecracks to Xarabat like expletives to sufferers of Tourettes syndrome? But his stoicism revived me and I began to hack at the ground, marking out the perimeter of our grave as directed by the Doctor. Focusing on the labour helped stave off the worst of the terror, and as I swung and heaved and lifted my tool, I prayed that our torturers would not take off their masks. As long as they were faceless there was hope.

Chapter 12

While our shadows shortened, for some time the thuds of our spades slicing earth and discarding it were the only sounds we heard, apart from the occasional sharp cry of a bird of prey hovering above us and the intermittent mutterings of the Doctor. Cadaverous and crow-like, the Pharmacist remained still and silent, observing us with one black-gloved hand resting on his weapon.

Our grave was about a metre deep when we heard a low, thunderous rumble in the sky which grew louder with each second. We looked up to see two hawkish shapes appear through the blue of the cloudless sky as their war cry resounded, ripping through the landscape. I glanced round; the Pharmacist was staring upwards, apparently frozen to the spot. The Doctor, who had huge blobs of perspiration dripping from his eyebrows, was shaking his arm and urging him to run. I looked at Xarabat, who held his index finger upwards. He means one, I thought. I hoped he was wrong.

The Doctor was the first to run. The Pharmacist started to follow then stopped, took off his AK-47, looked back and aimed it towards us. The Doctor screamed something and he turned and fled too, overtaking the Doctor just before the hill descended. I flung down my spade, ready to flee, but was obstructed by Xarabat gripping me round the waist with his arms in a determined bear hug, and toppling us both into the hole we had dug for ourselves.

"Lie face down," he said, placing the head of my spade over my own, so that the handle formed a wooden spine down my back, and reached for his spade to position it in the same way on himself. "Never thought I'd be grateful for these big boys, did you?" he said, a moment before any more speech would be drowned.

The fighter jets swooped, each dropping two loads. The earth shook beneath and around us, throwing up clumps of dirt and stones that landed on our bodies, until with a final shudder it settled and laid to rest once more. We lay listening with our hands over our ears to the fading drone of the warplanes. I felt the weight lifting from me as Xarabat removed my spade and told me to sit up. For a few minutes we sat coughing out soil and grit, picking out bits that had found their way into our ears and nostrils.

At Xarabat's suggestion we crawled along the ground to the edge of the hill where we could look down on the compound below. From there we could see that all the vehicles were burnt-out, wrecked shambles, and the few concrete buildings, including our former jail, had been destroyed. There was no sign of life.

We took our time descending the slope; cautious and alert, looking out for any movements, listening for sounds of survival. The road the compound led into was deserted and pebbled with fallout from the explosion. As we turned into the yard, we had to walk round a large crater which the crumpled digger had half fallen into. It appeared to have taken the Doctor with it. We could see his face sticking out at one end of its jaws, his legs protruding from the other end. I stared at his pulped, gory crown and his spattered features, and wondered what had happened to his balaclava.

Beyond the crater, we saw that the Pharmacist's fate was no better. We identified him by one of his boots jutting out from slabs of concrete. The one arm we could see was still holding the handle of his Kalashnikov which had been broken in two. His face and the remains of his body were hidden under the mound of the pulverised structure that had been his headquarters. If any of the other jihadists had been sheltering there during the air raid we were certain they were dead.

Xarabat pointed to a corner of the yard. Sprawled on the top of a pyramid of broken, tossed pallets, the Belgian teen lay; a lifeless dummy. With his arms splayed out he reminded me of a Guy Fawkes, the ones we used to make when I was a boy, to throw on the bonfire.

"Poor kid," Xarabat said, holding the orange boiler suit he had just removed to my face, to mop up my tears. "You'd better get yours off quick too. You don't want to be looking like one of those traffic lollipop things."

"A beacon."

"Yeah, that's the one. You don't want to be looking like a beacon."

He walked towards the crater, peered into it and shocked me by jumping in. A pair of sandals landed on the ground in front of my bare and blistered feet, from which I had peeled off the torn, clay-clumped socks I had been forced to dig in.

"These will come to good use," he said.

"Oh Christ. You don't mean I'm going to have to walk in the Doctor's shoes?"

Xarabat laughed and bent down again.

"I don't think there's anything we can do for him now," I said, when I saw Xarabat heaving, shifting the teeth of the digger away from the smashed corpse.

"It's what he can do for us, brother," Xarabat said, holding up a pistol.

"Seriously? Where did he keep that hidden?"

"Under his plus-size dress."

Xarabat climbed out of the pit, wiped the pistol with my discarded boiler suit and put it down on the ground. He began unstrapping my sandals from his feet. He threw them over to me and slipped on the Doctor's sandals.

"Bit gay, but just my size."

Out of the compound, on the open road flanked by wasteland, we felt exposed and at the same time protected by the absence of buildings and vehicles. Around the corner was a different scene. Ahead of us, spaced out on either side of the road were various buildings; some intact, some collapsed and some completely ruined. Beyond those, there was a more densely built-up area which we presumed was residential. A beat-up car and two motorcycles passed by without paying us any attention as we reached a large building. Xarabat said it was a bakery, which was closed; whether permanently or for the day I had no way of knowing. Next to it was a warehouse with half of its walls missing, the other half precarious, with panels caving in.

My first reaction when I saw a British ambulance nosing through the gap between the bakery and the warehouse was to feel relief. The driver, who was wearing a white helmet, called to us through the window, but my instinctive urge to run towards him was restrained by Xarabat crossing my chest with his arm. In his other hand he held up the Doctor's pistol.

"Wait, I don't trust them."

The ambulance driver shouted something in Arabic.

"He says he has been sent to rescue you," Xarabat said.

Behind me I heard more words spoken in Arabic. Xarabat dropped his gun and put his hands up. Another man in a white helmet stepped in front of us, pointing a rifle at Xarabat's chest. The driver hopped out of the ambulance and ran towards us, jabbering and waving a mobile phone. The only word which made any sense to me, which he kept repeating, was 'Gilly.' Smiling and pointing at the phone, he put it to my ear. "Dylan, Dylan are you there?"

Clearing my throat and squeezing my eyes with my fingers, I took hold of the phone. My voice was reduced to a croak as I answered.

"Gilly?"

"Yes, it's really me. Are you okay Dylan? Are you okay, bro?"

"I'm okay. What's going on with these guys?"

"Listen. They are sound, just do what they say and I'll explain everything later. They've been sent to bring you back and it shouldn't take long. We're all waiting for you at the Turkish border."

Repeating what I had just heard to Xarabat, I handed the phone back to the driver who gesticulated towards the ambulance, indicating that we should get in it. He made an attempt to give me an explanation, but it soon became clear that he had few words of English. Xarabat interpreted for him and he seemed to appreciate my friend's value. Xarabat and I were put in the back of the ambulance and the second Syrian climbed into the front with the driver.

The journey was fast and shorter than I remembered; during my ordeal I had lost any sense of geography and forgotten how close we were to Turkey. Without a blindfold, through the windows in the back of the ambulance doors I caught flashes of skeletal houses and shops. Xarabat translated a few of the many slogans painted in Arabic letters on walls, billboards and posters for me, until I got the gist of the ideology behind them. Then the territory began to look more familiar, and I recognised the bustling normality of Bab Al Hawa border town.

Xarabat and I crouched on the floor as we passed through the border crossing. Our progress seemed quick; for a few minutes we moved slowly and after a brief halt we were on our way. Moments later we stopped again. This time the ambulance door was slid open. The driver held out a hand for us to step down, while his colleague directed us to the glass door of the office building we had parked in front of. They led us through into the main reception area, where a dapper, middle-aged man in a business suit greeted us in Turkish. He stepped forward to shake everyone's hand, and led Xarabat and me into a corridor where he knocked on a door and waited.

Hearing a response to a voice within, he opened the door and waved his hand for me to enter, then held it up with a smile to stop Xarabat following me. I had no time to feel concern as I took in the scene. In front of me with their arms held out, grinning and calling my name, were Gilly and Atif. Behind them were three female figures dressed in black headscarves and abayas, moving forward with radiant smiles. As they came into focus through my tears, I realised they were Freya, Em and Saffi. Standing back, behind a desk, was a short, sandy-haired man dressed in jeans, a white shirt and a leather sports jacket which matched his tan shoes. He watched with a detached air, as I was kissed and embraced in turn. When we were a little calmer he came out from behind his desk and held out his hand to me.

Gilly took on the role of introducing him.

"Dylan, this is Hugo Brimble-Goggin. He's a representative from the Foreign Office, and kind of the liaison man with the Sham Civil Guard guys. You know, the ones who rescued you."

I shook the official's hand.

"He's going to have a word with you, and take you to the Counter Terrorism Police officer who has come to give you a debriefing before we can leave. Have I got that right?"

Hugo Brimble-Goggin bowed his head. Gilly turned back to me.

"They said it shouldn't take long so we're hoping to be out of here within a couple of hours. But first there's something I promised to do which should only take a few minutes."

Gilly walked up to a chair by the side of the room where I was surprised to see the bags containing my camera and equipment.

"This is the deal, Dylan. I promise everything will be explained to you when we get to the holiday villa, hopefully by tonight, if all goes well. We are just going to re-enact the scene of you arriving in the ambulance so I can film it. The others all know what to do, so all you have to do is get out of the ambulance, act as if you've just seen us again for the first time, and make a big deal of the White Hats, showing gratitude for saving you and all that."

"What about Xarabat?" I said.

"Who?"

I explained to Gilly who Xarabat was.

"Well," he said, "he's not going to be included in this scene but we'll ask where he is when we're done. The sooner we get this over with the quicker we'll get out of here."

The two Syrians were waiting by the ambulance smoking when we came out. The filming was efficient and effortless. I performed exactly as instructed, and the driver took over the camera when it was Gilly's turn to embrace me in in the act of reunion. Brimble-Goggin, who had been observing our performance, walked over to shake the White Hats hands, speaking to them in Turkish. This time Em translated when they replied in the same language.

"They are saying you must promise to put it in the film how they rescued you."

Gilly and I nodded and put our thumbs up.

"Tamam, Tamam," Em said.

"Tell them I genuinely am very grateful," I said. "Thank you, thank you," I called to them as we waved them off in the ambulance.

There were two more male strangers waiting to meet me when we got back into the reception area. One was Em's Turkish cousin, a tall, nervous young man wearing skinny jeans and a Metallica T-shirt. "This is my cousin Mahmut, Dylan. He has to leave now but he wanted to be introduced to you. I told him we will speak on Skype tomorrow. He's been absolutely wonderful, and he's played a big part in getting you out of there."

I realised he must speak good English so I told him I was grateful from the bottom of my heart.

"I look forward to speaking to you tomorrow," I said, embracing him as he left.

The other man introduced himself as Peter Bridgeford from the British Counter Terrorism Unit. He congratulated me on my timely release.

"I have a number of questions I am required to ask you about your kidnapping and the actors involved, before I can release you. But I hope it will not take too long."

"No problem, but first can you tell me what has happened to Xarabat, the Kurdish guy who was in the prison with me? I don't think I would have survived without him, and I really want to know he's going to be safe."

"Well, I think I can reassure you on that score. He is in the very capable hands of my American colleague, Perry Burke, from the Envoy's office."

At that moment, the door opposite the one we were about to enter opened, and a huge, burly man with rosacea-flushed cheeks strode out with Xarabat.

"Speaking of the devil," Bridgeford said, planting a friendly slap on Perry Burke's hulky bicep.

Xarabat grinned in response to my enquiring look.

"Don't worry about me," he said, "I'm going to be taken care of and everything is going to be all right. I've got your mobile number and your email address, so I'll be in touch as soon as I can." He winked. "And remember to check out my cousin as soon as you get back to Mancaster, okay? Get a free haircut." He slapped my hand as he walked away, dwarfed by the big American.

"Speak soon, brother. Stay safe," I called down the corridor.

My friends waited in the reception area while Bridgeford interrogated me about locations, names, descriptions of personal and physical characteristics, the ethnicities of the jihadists, the languages they spoke and any references they had made to their homelands. He was very interested in Shaki, but I said I saw no evidence that he was anything other than the humanitarian he claimed to be. Of course, I had the most to say about the two Brits, and Bridgeford told me they had significant intelligence on the pair, which my report matched.

At four in the afternoon he let me go, which delighted my girlfriend and friends, because it meant we had sufficient time to get to Hatay airport for the six o'clock flight they had booked seats on.

"Em is going to call a minibus now to take us," Freya said. "We couldn't book a seat for you obviously, but we've checked and there are plenty of empty ones available, so we should be okay. Atif and Saffi are flying to Istanbul to meet Jamal. They'll stay there overnight and fly back to the UK tomorrow. Ro and Ash are going to meet us at Antalya airport. It takes about an hour to get there from Hatay."

On the way to the car park to meet the minibus I teased the girls about their dress.

"So what's all this about? I didn't recognise you at first."

"Let's just say some of the characters we had to deal with were very conservative," said Em, laughing.

"Don't worry," Freya said, "all will be revealed when we get to the villa."

I whispered in her ear, tugging at the sleeve of her black gown.

"You could start by revealing what's underneath that."

Without answering me, Freya whisked off her headscarf and pulled up and off the loose abaya, draping them on a bicycle rack by the wall, followed by Em, and Saffi who kept her hijab on, just as the minibus pulled up.

Chapter 13

At the airport, the smooth transaction of the purchase of my airline ticket I attributed to a telephone call, made in advance of my arrival by Hugo Brimble-Goggin, which I learnt about from the lady staffing the desk. Although I had cleaned myself up a little in the bathroom at the border offices, I was still wearing the grimy, soil-streaked T-shirt and sweat pants from the grave. We had decided the priority was to get my seat booked first, before changing into the fresh top and shorts Freya had brought for me. Despite my appearance, the lady was charming and helpful, and allocated us seats as close together as she could.

The only time Freya had let go of my hand since we were re-united was to pass through the passport and security controls. As soon as we were seated next to each other on the plane, she nestled in as close to me as she could. We were quiet for most of the hour-long flight to Antalya, with Freya stroking my hand and sneaking gentle little kisses on my chin. It was good, although it felt strange, to bask in a little adoration. We had agreed to save any discussion about the events of the previous four days until we were all together in the privacy of the holiday villa. The longest conversation Freya and I had on the plane was about a technique she offered to teach me.

"It's a kind of acupressure for the emotions without needles, called Tapping. There's been research on it, it's worked really well with sufferers of post-traumatic stress disorder such as army veterans.

"Well, I'm not sure I've got PTSD. Maybe, but I'm really lucky to get out of that madness after only a few days."

"Okay, but I'll show you these Emotional Freedom Techniques just in case anything comes up."

"You're all the therapy I need," I said, kissing her on the lips.

It seemed too soon to say goodbye to Atif and Saffi when we had passed through Customs at Antalya airport.

"Take care, bro," I said, holding Atif, reluctant to let him go. "I'll be in touch and we'll catch up soon. Freya and I will cook you and Saff a nice dinner."

Saffi began to cry, so Freya and I comforted her and asked her to give our love to Jamal in Istanbul. Then Ro's appearance in the Arrivals hall created another little whirlwind of emotion and excitement. We waved to our friends as they took the escalator for their domestic flight. Chattering and interrupting each other, we made our way to find Ro's hired car in the car park.

Knowing of the general good taste and penchant for luxury shared by both Ro and Ash, it was no surprise when we arrived at the villa that it was beautiful, well designed and equipped, and in a gorgeous location with a terrace overlooking the sea. Ash greeted us at the door, rattling a bottle of champagne in an ice bucket. He put it down to give us a more affectionate welcome, especially me, and took us on a tour of the house which ended on the terrace. He had placed candles all around on ledges and on the patio table in the centre, where six champagne glasses were waiting to toast my safe return, and the announcement of the official start of our holiday.

"We've ordered a delicious selection of the finest pide this town has to offer, for dinner," Ro said. "It's coming in about an hour, to give you time to have a bath and chill out if you want."

"That sounds fantastic," I said.

Freya and I took our champagne to the bedroom while she ran the bath for me, adding bubbles and oils she said were calming. Returning to the feast of perfect Turkish pizzas and cold Turkish beer in a thick cotton bath robe, refreshed and revived by a back massage from Freya, felt surreal.

Throwing our crusts into the boxes and reaching for more beers, we agreed with Gilly that it was a good time to

125

tell our stories. I began with a more vivid version of the account I had given to Bridgeford at the border. My use of colourful language and the anecdotes of Xarabat's humour made the darkest details more palatable, except the grave digging episode. Nothing quite took the edge off the horror of that.

"Go on, Em," Gilly said when I had finished answering their questions. "It's best if you start, and I'll tell him about the filming."

Em was thoughtful for a few minutes. "Right, I think we all get that this is a really emotional trip for us to relive what's happened this past week. So I'm just going to do my best to stick to the facts of what happened at our end. Okay, starting with Wednesday evening: Gilly and I were all packed and ready to catch the flight here on Thursday morning, when Freya called with the news that you'd been kidnapped. It was about five o'clock, so seven here. At first we were just so upset and panicked we really didn't know what to do, then I had the idea of contacting my Turkish relatives. I didn't have a clue about what they could do either, I was just desperate for anything that might help you. First I made a Skype call with my grandmother. She said she thought her nephew, my cousin Mahmut, had a friend who had relatives in Idlib province where you were captured. She got in touch with him right away and he Skyped me straight back. I told him about the convoy, about you, and what Atif had told us. Mahmut said he would see if he could speak to his friend, and would call me as soon as he had something to tell me. I think it was about ten o'clock that night when he came on Skype again to let me know his friend had made enquiries. A cousin of his in the Sham Civil Guard knew who was holding you, and your rough whereabouts. We were so hopeful, we made a quick decision to get a flight from Antalya on Thursday morning and go to my grandmother's village in Hatay."

Em explained that her grandmother and other members of her extended family were thrilled about her visit, having not seen her since she was a little girl.

"It was such a delight to meet them and spend some time with them, not just talking over the Internet. But we were so distraught about you. I've promised them another visit in Spring next year."

"I'd really love to see them again too," Freya said. "And I'm sure Atif and Saffi feel the same. It was so good of your aunties and uncles to put us all up, and look after us while we were waiting for news about Dylan. Everyone in the family was so lovely."

"Obviously." Em laughed and continued. "Anyway, before we had even got on the flight to Turkey something very weird and wonderful happened."

"Go on," I said.

"I don't think you could make this up, could you Gilly? Gilly and I were messing about in the Duty-Free shop, testing the most expensive stuff, like you do. A man, who was picking up a bottle of outrageously dear aftershave, did a double take and looked at us. You'll never guess who it was. It was Bron Pearson and he recognised us from Milly's inquest. He asked how we were all doing, which made me burst into tears when I thought about you. He insisted on taking us into the VIP bar, buying us drinks and finding a little corner where we could tell him about what happened. We didn't have very much time to talk, maybe half an hour. Bron said he split his time between the States and England now, because he's landed a juicy post as a presenter of an American news and politics chat show. He was on his way to Istanbul to meet up with his wife and some friends to take a short holiday in Cappadocia. He gave us his contact details, and told us to Skype or FaceTime him when we got to Hatay to give him some news, because he wanted to help in any way he could."

"Bron Pearson." I repeated his name; incredulous.

"Yes. But listen, here's the thing. When I met Mahmut, who speaks brilliant English by the way, he wanted to know all about you; what you did and all of that. I told him about you and Gilly wanting to start your own company using your journalistic and film skills. He asked me what we would do if they wanted money for you, like a few million pounds or something. That's when I mentioned Bron Pearson. I said I had no reason to think he'd pay a ransom, but he was a rich and successful celebrity with contacts in the US and UK, so maybe he could do something."

I laughed, it was too much. "Oh my God."

"Wait, it gets wilder. So my cousin goes and relates all this to his friend, who tells his relative in Syria. He discusses it with his guys, and by eight o'clock on Thursday night they had a proposal to put to us, well Gilly and Bron really."

"I always had a bit of a soft spot for Bron," Ro said, bringing in a fresh batch of beers, "Suspected that deep down he wasn't such a bad guy."

"We owe him for this, that's for sure," Gilly said, adding that it was a good time for him to take up the story if Em wanted him to. "So what their deal boiled down to was that if we agreed to make a documentary film to support their cause, with backing from Pearson, they would make sure you were freed. They said we could begin with the story of the convoy and your kidnap, then some scenes recording their role in the conflict and at the end, your rescue by them."

"Wait a minute, what cause? Whose cause?" I said.

"I've written down the name of the Islamist group that Yusuf, the cousin of Mahmut's friend, is involved with. Rebels, opposition fighters. I can never remember it because I can't pronounce it. Mahmut says they keep changing it anyway."

"So Pearson agreed to all this?"

"He did. Amazing, eh? Not only that, when Em and I

Facetimed him after Mahmut had told us about Yusuf's proposal, he didn't even hesitate. He said that he'd transfer the ten grand they wanted upfront to Gilly on Friday morning first thing, and said that he was willing to invest more in our production company so that we could get on with editing, putting out the film and promoting it. He also promised that when he got back to the States he'd see what he could do at his end to get it noticed."

I placed my hands on the crown of my head and shook it. "Oh man. Oh man. What's the catch?"

"I knew you'd like that bit, not sure about some of the other details. There's not exactly a catch, but wait until I tell you about the scenes we filmed and what they said they wanted from us."

"Sounds like a catch. You mean to tell me you already did the filming in less than two days?"

"We actually did it this morning, and I transferred the money to Yusuf as soon as we got the word from Brimble-Goggin that you'd arrived at the Border office. On Thursday night Mahmut told Yusuf that Pearson had given the go-ahead for funding the film. He said that's when Yusuf's gang got really excited; it became more about the association with the celebrity and the publicity rather than the money. Early on Friday morning Em and I spoke with Yusuf on Skype, with Mahmut translating for us. Yusuf said we had to act quickly because there were two doctors who had been working with their own team, filming in the Idlib countryside. They were willing to support and play a role in our film, but were due leave Turkey on Saturday, this afternoon. We had to get up at five this morning because Yusuf arranged for me and Mahmut to be picked up with the equipment at six, by someone he called a friend. Yusuf's guy, Hadi, could speak some English and drove us to the location where they wanted to film, somewhere on the outskirts of Reyhanli. Hadi took us to a half bombed-out school where we were introduced to two White Hats, two armed men, a European-looking man with a walkie-talkie and the doctors; a Syrian-British male and a Syrian-American female who said they were ex-military."

"Did you get to meet their team?"

"No, they said they were working in another part of the building. The doctors were waiting for us in a classroom that had been turned into some kind of field hospital. Hadi said that the White Hat with the camera would help me with filming if I needed it. He said that all I needed to do was film the scenes they asked me to, so I could tell the world what was happening in this war. I had to promise to say good things about them, and of course how you'd been saved by them at the end."

"Is that all?" I said.

Gilly cast me a sheepish glance. "To be honest, everything happened so quickly, I just thought it was best to ask no questions and get on with the job. I had to follow the direction of the guy with a walkie-talkie. I waited at the entrance of the school building with the two guys with Kalashnikovs. I didn't hear aircraft but there were some explosions close by and smoke began gushing out of a side street. I ran through the schoolyard and the gates to film an ambulance screeching past the school. When it stopped, two more White Hats jumped out and ran towards the rubble at the side of the school building. They began shouting, lifting up and throwing away bits of concrete and digging with their hands. From nowhere, one appeared with what looked like a baby in his arms. I was trying to shoot him, but he was running so fast the footage isn't great. Then Walkie-Talkie Guy shouted at me to go back to the schoolyard. Another ambulance came in. A man, screaming and holding his face, was helped out on a stretcher and taken into the clinic. I followed him inside, and filmed him and a woman holding a baby that wasn't crying or anything. The male doctor began speaking to the camera, giving a commentary regarding the victims he was about to treat, with the help of the other doctor and a male nurse who had joined them. He said there had been a bomb attack from a Syrian regime plane which appeared to have dropped some incendiary weapon, because people were suffering from severe burns. Several male teenagers staggered into the room, with torn clothing and what appeared to be scorched flesh hanging from their bodies. At a signal from my director, they began flailing their arms and moaning. Then I was told to go out again to the yard to film the man I saw arriving, as he climbed back in the ambulance with white cream smothered on his face."

"It doesn't sound right, somehow," I said. "Was it for real? Did they call it a reconstruction or what?"

"Not exactly, but they acted as if I should accept it as a real incident."

"So that's the catch. They want to control the narrative."

"Look, Dylan. Can you understand that I didn't care, because the most important thing to me was that you stayed alive. To be honest, I was shitting it."

I reached over to put my hand on the back of my friend's neck and pulled him over to me.

"Aw, mate, I'm sorry. I have no words to let you know how grateful I am for what you've done for me, and how totally happy I am to be with you all. Okay, enough for now," I said, releasing him. "There'll be time enough to look at the footage and talk about how we're going to do this. In the meantime, we've got some serious celebrating and catching up on the holiday to do."

I lifted up my beer bottle to show I intended to be cheery. Supping it, I walked over to the edge of the terrace to listen to the shushing of the sea, and watch the rainbows of lights from bars flicker through the prisms of its ripples.

Freya came behind me and took my hand.

"For now, I just want to say this," I said, standing before them when she led me back to the group. "Whatever this film is going to be, it can only be our version of the truth. Maybe a fraction of lots of different truths, if that makes sense. One day I'd like to go back to Syria, to see the amazing country and meet The People. Can you believe that apart from Xarabat the only Syrians I met were a few White Hats?"

They shook their heads. Gilly passed me a beer. I sat down.

"It seems to me that there are too many foreign fingers in the shit pie that is the Syrian war. Well, my truth, however broken and battered it may come stumbling into the picture, at least has survived to tell the tale. And it will not be a lie."

If you enjoyed this, read the opening pages from:

Stalkbook by Pamela Turton

Saturday, October 31st 2015

Lurker. Lurker. Stalker. Stalker. I've got this. I'm recording. We are live. We are live. Listen. Cops. Nine, nine, nine. What's your emergency? That's right. Run away from me. Run away you worthless. Worthless. Anyway, I've got you. On here. The whole world will see. You. Stalking. Me.

No. No. Stop shouting. Is it me, hoofing? Striking the cobbles like my spooked pony? Not ready to jump. Woah. Woah. My feet are made of cork. I'm floating. Jesus. Jesus. Walking on water. The earth is moving. No floor under my feet. Shallow abyss. Crashing.

Crash landing! Bent the wrong way. What's the crack? Bone? My ankle? No. A hundred pounds-worth of heel snapped off. What will he say? If it were up to me, I'd have my riding boots on. Not these. Heels for him. Ha. Fancy dress. Get off your knees. Grit's ripping my skin. Could do without these clothes. Coat twisting around. Trapping me. Something pulling. Scarf a strangler. Grab the wall. Up, up. Now I'm lop-sided. A wonky cripple. A wobbly toy clown.

My 'phone. My 'phone. Feel around. Can't have gone far. Take the glove off. Oh, shit. I'm in it. Hands shaking. Makes it worse. Kneading dough. Sponge fingers. Disgusting dog foul. God, not on my face. Can't stop the retch. Pool of sick. On top.

Move away. Move away. Find the 'phone. Look for the light. Not the lights passing through me. Misty circles glowing. Growing behind my eyes. Stinking black cauldron. Swirling. Dirty water boiling. Gas bubbling white. Exploding. Steam rising. Turning green.

Dragging. Too slow. Too dark. Clods of purple earth.

Rolling near the mouth, the tunnel. Blades of grass sprouting glass splinters. Biting things are here. Hands jerking. Cardboard hitting hard brick. It's a cave. I am a troll. Making horrible echoes. Cats. Rats. Bats. Leaking out like treacle. Webs grid my eyes. I see like a fly. My heart is a drum. Bum, bum. Faster, faster. What's that? Listen. The devil is playing. The witch is still stalking. I hear her wicked orchestra. Moving her on. Howls. Screams. Laughing. At me. Inside me. Horror movie. Nightmare noises. Wake up. Wake up.

Gilly

Saturday, 26th September 2015

This beauty under my hands took some talking into. Not exactly something I'd always yearned for. I was never short of a bike to ride. Taken for granted models gifted to me on birthdays and at Christmas. This one's different, in a class of its own; a key player-to-be in my plans. I'd had to think through my angle before I put it out to the old G. 'Thought you wanted me to have a healthy lifestyle? Get an interest, you know?'

'Thought that's what the gym membership I shelled out for was all about.'

'I know, Dad. Don't get me wrong, the gym's been great. I'm deffo keeping it up.' That was true. My enhanced buff-ness was noticed on Talkbook when I posted a few work-out selfies, with a jokey caption to play down how good I was looking, to be fair. Very Liked, ha. The under-lit pool with the starry ceiling, menthol oil evaporating in the steam room and cold showers has put me right after many a messy night. Not to mention the massages. Georgia asking what she can do for me, wondering what I can do for her I'm sure. The idea that I should test Dad out for a personal trainer occurred to me, then the thought that was best shelved for the time being. Mental note. Maybe Minky, the new girl who takes clients - trainees - out to the small city parks and canal paths?

'Anyway Dad, this is different. Look, I'm really grateful for the gym, you know?' Grateful was a word I had to remember to use a lot. It went a long way. 'Gym keeps me fit and focused.' That is actually true. Working out has become routine now. The bike is a new, edgy, useful extra. 'But I need the bike to get around town, uni and all that. And if, like, when I find a job.' Job, another helpful word to throw in.

'What sort of job?'

'Not sure yet. Something that'll tie in with my Advertising degree maybe.' Verbal shrug. I wasn't convincing myself, let alone him.

'Thought that's what the car was for.'

'Aww, Dad. Mate. You know how much that car means to me.' Straight up. Mercedes CLA Sports. The one I wanted. He could have said no. Still, it was for my eighteenth and it reflects on him, doesn't it, the wheels I drive? 'Thing is, a bike's much easier to nip around the centre, campus and all that. Saves money too.' I ignored the sardonic chuckles, raspberry-blowing and mild profanity coming from Dad. 'Got to think of the environment too,' I said. That last point was a mistake. Knew as soon as it came out.

He stopped laughing. 'Since when did you give a bloody monkey's about the environment, son?'

'You'd be surprised, Dad, Getting hard to ignore these days, don't you think?' Not the best spin to take with him so I moved on. 'I'm hoping to get involved in the social side of things, actually. There's a Spring Charity Cycle Run I want to get involved with.'

Haw-haw-haw. Pause. Good sign; the Old G. was thinking. 'To be honest, that's not a bad reason either. Goes down well to have that kind of image when you're in business, you know. Look at me.' He reminded me of all the good works he made time for. Dad, the reluctant philanthropist pillar, putting out for needy people and projects he has less than a passing interest in. 'Not all about sales you know. Folks got to trust you. Polish up your reputation with your skills.'

'You're right, Dad.'

With the marching beat of Drake's 'Headlines' taking over my head through my earphones, I can only feel the jounce and bounce of my new wheels over the resisting cobblestones. The rain scatters silver and gold on the pavements; light from the apartment windows reflecting, like silent fragments of fireworks on the witches' brew oozing from the canal basin. Magical even though it's often rancid, it makes money for the developers. Location, location. In winter it boils and simmers; molten granite and black marble. It bubbles with varying degrees of murk and green in other seasons; verdigris and rust. Best not to think of the floaters and sinkers; weighted carcasses, human and animal, innocents, un-whole criminals, toppled drunks and junkies. Pretty, trusting ducklings, beautiful, snotty-nosed swans, frogs, newts and uglier things live here too.